From The Women's Press Ltd
34 Great Sutton Street, London EC1V 0DX

D0625150

The Women's Press
science fiction

The Women's Press science fiction series features new titles by contemporary writers and reprints of classic works by well-known authors. Our aim is to publish science fiction by women and about women; to present exciting and provocative feminist images of the future that will offer an alternative vision of science and technology, and challenge male domination of the science fiction tradition itself.

We hope that the series will encourage more women both to read and to write science fiction, and give the traditional science fiction readership a new and stimulating perspective.

JANE PALMER

Jane Palmer was born in 1946 and lives in Bedfordshire. She works as a freelance artist. *The Watcher* is her second science fiction novel; her first, *The Planet Dweller*, was published in The Women's Press Science Fiction Series in 1985.

About *The Planet Dweller*:

'Jane Palmer's first novel comically (and Britishly) juxtaposes menopausal female reality with a farcical chauvinist sf subplot' *The Guardian*

'Quite unashamedly a good sci-fi adventure . . . cleverly weaves together all the ingredients for a good read' *Chartist*

'An exuberant send-up of some of the wilder eccentricities of both the sf genre and real life' *City Limits*

'*The Planet Dweller* appropriates all the furniture of TV sci-fi and duly stands it on its head . . . thoroughly satisfying' Mary Gentle, *Interzone*

JANE PALMER

THE WATCHER

The Women's Press
sf

First published by The Women's Press Limited 1986
A member of the Namara Group
34 Great Sutton Street, London EC1V 0DX

British Library Cataloguing in Publication Data

Palmer, Jane
The watcher.
I. Title
823'.914[F]   PR6066.A44/

ISBN 0-7043-4038-0

Typeset by MC Typeset Limited, Chatham, Kent
Printed and bound in Great Britain
by Hazell, Watson & Viney Ltd, Aylesbury, Bucks
Member of the BPCC Group

Acknowledgments

I would like to acknowledge the assistance of astronomer Andrea Prestwich, for whose advice on certain passages I am indebted; any errors incurred in my flights of fancy, however, are entirely my own.

The term 'per', which I use to denote the neutral gender, was invented by Marge Piercy in *Woman on the Edge of Time* (The Women's Press, 1979).

1

The stars sparkled through the dense atmosphere during the few moments of darkness as the yellow sun set, before the other appeared above the horizon. In those few moments Controller Opu shut down the refractor that had been deflecting the nutritional light waves from the setting sun into the energy pool below. The rising star's pink light had no nourishment value. Its luminosity was just as great, bathing everything in a pretty pallor, but it was the yellow sun which had given the ancient races the energy they needed to carry on industrious lives.

Three million years ago, the first refractor able to collect and store the sun's energy had been built (or so it was believed, because any trace of it had vanished long ago) and this had given the planet's most advanced life form the impetus it needed to evolve rapidly. Since then, the efficiency of these practical temples to Ojalie advancement had increased a thousandfold. Unfortunately, Ojalie ambition had not. The greatest delight of these edifices to their eyes was the way they spangled the planet with gigantic silver domes.

Opu tucked her long wings comfortably by her sides. Looking over her blunt beak, which ran seamlessly down from her cranium, she pondered on the glinting shields that were slowly closing as the pink sun rose above the horizon. 'Where would the Ojalie be now without those massive pools of light energy to bathe in when they felt they needed a little boost?' she wondered. 'Perhaps using their wings to soar above the cloud banks to collect their nourishment on the rare occasions the yellow sun disappeared behind them. Or perhaps chewing different plants to see if they could digest them.' The last thought was pretty silly because they had never developed any bowels to cope with such food, just a small mouth leading to a narrow throat connected to a digestive tract and bladder designed to deal only with liquid. This liquid was a mineral-rich fluid which bubbled from the crust of their planet, the only other form of nutrition they required, though over the millennia some other potions had been invented. These were only consumed for the pleasurable feelings they gave, and were responsible for more mid-air collisions than freak air currents.

Most of the space inside the short, wide-hipped bodies of the Ojalie was needed to allow their large-skulled offspring to grow. Their pelvic girdles were so wide they were unable to walk very well, but their wings more than compensated for this. It had probably never occurred to anyone that there would have been any pleasure in walking very far anyway. As the Ojalie were hermaphrodite, this shape was pretty standard, even between different racial types that had not interbred. Everyone had the ability to both inseminate and give birth. Without that exchange of genes they would never have been able to reach such a pitch of evolution.

Opu looked down at the chattering bundle of unco-ordinated wings, arms and legs, tumbling about the floor beneath everyone's feet, and wondered what pitch of evolution she was likely to represent. Her child had just managed to escape for the fifth time from the play-pen that was supposed to be child-proof, and was about to bite the leg of another of the control room staff in discovery of the different things a beak could be used for. If Opu had known how lively Opuna was going to be and how many friends she was going to lose, she would have thought twice about having her. Her gene partner, Anapa, had not so long ago looked thoughtfully at the antics of the bundle of disruption and observed, 'How does she manage to be so active? Mine hardly moves about at all.'

'Swap?' Opu had suggested hopefully.

'Not now I've got my home just how I like it,' was the prompt reply. 'But I might let you visit us when she runs out of energy and she has more control over her hands and beak.'

'A fine parent you are.'

'Maybe, but I'm sure you've more genes in her than I have.'

Knowing Anapa's disposition to be about as vivacious as the grey-skinned fungus-eating slow-worm, Opu had to agree.

The unfortunate control operator let out a shriek as the monster child's beak found her leg and she turned, only to find an innocent Opu looking as amazed as herself.

Finishing the shift, and coming under the frosty disapproval of her colleagues, Opu was able to tuck her squawking offspring beneath her short arm and fly back at a leisurely pace to the devastation of her own home. As things would immediately be dislodged and flung about as soon as she had tidied up, she had long since stopped bothering and only invited the most broad-minded of her friends in. She had thought about cutting down the amount of light nourishment she gave Opuna, but many who claimed to be more responsible had frowned severely at the idea. All growing children needed at least five meals every sun. Without it, they would shrivel up into nothing as their ancestors, so deprived, had done. Or just fall to pieces, as their experimental astronauts had done when they had travelled too far from the sun. The Ojalie were one of those many species dependent, like most vegetation, on their sun. The Ojalie had given up trying to leave their planet many years ago, but the old stories of what had happened to the early pioneers still made Opu shudder.

Perhaps her offspring would not be a pest forever. A long walk to try and tire Opuna into flying, only exhausted her and left the brat as ebullient as ever. They watched a golden-backed reptile disembowel an unsuspecting mollusc, then spit out its shell. Opu felt ill, while Opuna pondered the need to fly when such marvellous sights could be seen on the ground. 'Was I like her at that age?' Opu asked herself. At last she started to believe the horror stories her parent had told about her juvenile behaviour. They came upon an automatic cleanser scraping up the remains of some poor pulverised creature which had fallen from the sky. Opu decided Opuna's walk and flying lesson had lasted long enough. She scooped the brat up and, back home, placed her in the cubicle to be bathed in the life-giving sun's light, while she sprawled out and fanned herself with a wing. The one good thing about having a monster of a child was that it took her mind off other problems.

As Opu fanned her cares away she remembered the wispy shape she had imagined hovering over the refractor two shifts ago. She had put it down to the tiredness brought on by concentration and parenthood and, using this as an excuse, she talked Anapa into suffering the rigors of Opuna's delinquency while she took the other child of the union, Anop, who was far more docile.

That next shift she was able to place Anop in the play-pen built into the corner of the control room without having to worry whether she was about to engineer a disaster. Opu was therefore quite relaxed. Her colleagues had actually begun to speak to her again, and she no longer felt tired.

Then the scale showing the energy level suddenly dived. Only for a second, but enough for her to look out at the open shields to see a shape hovering menacingly over the energy pool. This time it was blazing intensely, like a miniature sun. Inside the spherical mass was a slowly changing amoebic shape, writhing this way and that in its flaming shell. It grew brighter and brighter with the energy it consumed.

'Vian Solran! Star Dancer!' one of the controllers shouted in alarm.

Instinctively Opu hit the lever which opened the power bank to the other stations dotted about the planet before the level could fall dangerously low.

'Vian Solran, Star Dancer . . .' Opu mused to herself when the emergency was over. It was strange how such ancient race memories could surface when someone was under stress. It was probably the most logical thing anyone could say about that energy vampire, though. For all their knowledge and expertise it might as well have been that star-devouring deity.

Legend had it that Vian Solran had been spewed out from a long dead quasar at the centre of the galaxy when it was young. In keeping with the character of its parent, the deity had developed the rapacious appetite of a collapsar. It was not pinned to just one position in space though. It could perform a deadly dance from one star to the next, devouring each in its turn.

That was the first visit. As yet, the visitor to Ojal had not yet become as ambitious as Vian Solran, but the unspoken fear that it was only a matter of time, grew. Long before the Star Dancer turned its attention to the suns themselves, the planet's energy pools would be bled dry, and the Ojalie would become extinct. Given their technical competence, however, no one had yet dared put that fear into words. Like a blip on the solar scan, or disease in the digestive tracts of the perverse creatures who decided to survive off vegetation, it had to be investigated.

The control room staff had been so stunned by that first sighting, they were not able to describe it when making out a report. Even the children could not invent words to express what they had seen, though Opu did not doubt for one moment that Opuna would have been able to.

Suggestions from every source of inventive knowledge tumbled in to explain the apparition seen by the staff of Main Base Station 93, usually such a lucid bunch. But no convincing explanation could be found. Monsters on Ojal were a thing of the remote past. They knew of no hostile civilisations wanting to attack their planet, though the Star Dancer must have been alien.

The only good thing to come of the ominous experience for Opu was that her gene partner now had to look after both children while she worked continuously with the other control staff in an attempt to trace the origin of the Star

5

Dancer, should it appear again. Even a small drain on an energy pool affected all the other stations, and there was a limit to how much they could subsidise each other.

As though it knew they were waiting for it, the Star Dancer's next appearance was at a station on the other side of the planet. Although the staff had been told to expect a drain on the energy pool, they were watching for something other than beautiful. To their amazement, a ghostly butterfly floated over their shields, sucking power from the pool like nectar from a blossom.

It was about this time that the lives of Opu and her gene partner became even more complicated: Anapa's, because she was obliged to look after both children, monstrous and docile, indefinitely, and Opu's because she was computed as being the best controller to take charge of the situation and trace the source of the Star Dancer. A sudden promotion her easy-going nature could have done without.

Space travel might have been biologically impossible for the Ojalie, but transmitting signals at sophisticated frequencies was not. Unable to visually observe the sky because their planet was almost permanently lit by their two suns, curiosity had driven them to design spacecraft which could carry satellites far beyond their planet, to orbit with the comets. They achieved this not long after constructing the first refractors about three million years ago. Now they had the ability to see and track anything within the known universe. This was something many species who were able to travel space had not achieved. Their expertise, and a willingness to share it, had made them very popular with the rest of the galaxy. Which was just as well, because it was obvious they were going to need help as the number of power drains caused by Star Dancer's visits began to increase.

2

Opu was still unable to find a solution to the multi-shaped Star Dancer after its sixteenth visit but, because it was energy, it could be traced. Things were becoming critical, when the Controller devised a way of attaching a tracking signal to the tail of the marauding manifestation. When the opportunity to use it did arise, the signal only managed to follow the apparition as far as the edge of a double star system. At that point, the parcel of energy accelerated beyond the speed of light, and easily shook off the tracking signal. No one had been expecting this. Not many things were known to travel at the speed of thought. Opu was beginning to feel like a wrung-out beak warmer. She hustled a message round the planet to rally the technicians and enough power to send out a computerised impulse which could pursue the thing at the speed of thought. If it travelled any faster than that she resolved to let somebody else try their luck.

Waiting for the power units and computer to be assembled, it did not help Opu to receive a near hysterical message from Anapa, telling her that Opuna had succeeded in alienating most of her friends, and had sent the remainder into a near frenzy, not unlike her own, as they tried to relieve her of the menace for a few hours. Opu had other things on her mind.

As the computer signal was lined up and waiting for the thirsty apparition's next visitation, Opu began to feel a relieving numbness creep over her. At least it made the waiting easier. Every available satellite was programmed to track the impulse, across the universe if necessary. It would have been futile to ask assistance of any world until they knew where it would lead them, so all they could do was sit back.

Suddenly the Star Dancer was there. Hovering above Station 30 at the planet's equator. This time shaped like a long-legged insect draped in swirling robes. While the station's crew topped up the energy pool from other stations, halfway across the globe Opu transmitted the computer impulse and had it tracking the intruder before it began its rapid retreat into space. To her relief and amazement, this time it did not escape.

By the time the Star Dancer had reached the other side of the galaxy, reaching its destination in less than seconds, erratic snippets of information began to pour in from different monitors. There was no sensible sequence to their arrival and the jumble was fed into a computer to un-scramble: lists of figures measuring the planet's location, density, size and atmosphere. Other data came in pictures, some easy to comprehend, and again some that had to be mangled out in the computer before they could be under-stood. At least they could be sure the Star Dancer came from a planet and was not an emanation from some freak star—but the name stuck anyway.

Now it was possible to contact the planets in the location and glean more specific information about the neighbouring solar system. Having given up using electromagnetic radia-tion waves for communication millennia ago, the Ojalie were now able to make instantaneous contact across light years using a sophisticated computerised elementary particle system. Transmitting to anyone with receivers to pick up their signal, Opu was able to gather that their quarry was on the third planet of a yellow sun which appeared to have a small dim red companion. The world was inhabited by various life forms and some of its land mass was quite verdant.

A species capable of space exploration on the planet Taigal Rax in a neighbouring solar system had long been interested in the Star Dancer's world. As the Taigalians were principally aquatic, they were naturally more interested in the large body of water which covered most of the planet, which they had named Perimeter 84926, than the creatures that had managed to crawl out of it. As they believed the oceans of the Star Dancer's home must eventually cover the remaining land masses just as they had done on Taigal Rax, it seemed rational to them to know more about the evolving species in the water than the eventually-to-be-drowned ones out of it. They did send Opu some specific information, however.

A precocious land animal had evolved from one of several similar species, becoming reasonably intelligent. This animal and other larger life forms had only four limbs and there appeared to be two sexes. It had enough intelligence to launch a space vehicle carrying odd information about its planet and a small plaque to show what it looked like, with one of the larger sex making a sign of some sort with an upper limb. The creature was known to have a fear/aggression complex about its own kind, and to be terrified of anything out of its immediate experience. Any contact to be made with extreme caution, if at all.

'Very helpful,' Opu remarked out loud. 'Any signal from here is definitely out.'

'No chance they could be sending the creature deliberately, if they are aggressive?' somebody suggested.

'With their backward technology?' sniffed Opu without even bothering to look away from the monitor to see who had spoken. 'No way.'

She sat back and thought. Their only chance lay with the aquatic species on Taigal Rax who were so interested in this planet's oceans. They knew many details about the creatures inhabiting Perimeter 84926, and were closer to it than any other comparable intelligent life. They even had laboratories deep in its crust and slumbering service robots at the bottom of its oceans ready to take simple instructions and feed information back. Hardly had she finished the thought, than Opu was transmitting a detailed summary of their predicament to Taigal Rax.

She sent out next for android engineers. She wanted them to design a mechanism with the ability to track the Star

Dancer on its own planet. As soon as her intentions were known, the chorus of controllers, who secretly thought they could do the job better, arose. 'But there isn't time . . .'

'There will be,' Opu assured them without further elaboration. 'Somebody find me Controller Annac and bring her here.'

'But she's dead . . . or retired . . .'

Unable to breathe in the hothouse of objectors, Opu unfurled her wings and stepped out on to the balcony where she took off into the cool pink sky without a word of explanation or apology.

She glided over the rambling twisted homes that unevenly punctuated the skyline in a haphazard fashion, floating over spacious gardens dotted with the occasional residence. The older people lived here, out of the flight paths of the younger more reckless fliers, and whiled away their time doing anything that age, advanced technology and their fancy allowed. Opu's purple-scaled tunic was quite imposing as she hovered over the flat roof of one home, catching the attention of the figure seated on it.

'Thought it about time you retired too, young Opu?' Controller Annac asked.

'I am tired of promotion, children and monstrous apparitions that drop in from the other side of the galaxy,' she agreed as she touched down on the limited space beside Annac.

'So you should retire. Though I thought you went in for a youngster. What's she like?'

'A brat.'

'Oh. Some are you know.'

'Problem with retiring, though, is that . . .' Opu took a deep breath and stopped.

'Is that?'

'Is that nobody else will be living to retirement age if you can't help me with a small problem,' Opu managed to say without sounding too overcome at the thought of it herself.

Annac looked up from the plan she had been analysing.

'I wouldn't call that a small problem. What do you want me to do?'

'A long while ago you devised a system for transmitting certain forms of matter from one place to another at a speed faster than light without the need for a receiver.'

Annac gave her a long hard look with her large orange eyes.

'You mean the one which used the Kybini particle?'

'That's it. The elementary particle without any mass.'

'I withdrew the proposal for the Kybini System.'

'I know,' said Opu.

'Then you know why.'

'I do. But it is not my intention to use it to transmit people.'

'Even if I am sure you won't, how can I be sure no one else will?' the older Ojalie demanded. 'Mineral matter was what it was intended for, not us.'

'You can be sure very few of us will ever be doing anything again if you don't let me have it,' Opu said with enough gravity to make Annac bend her moral stance.

'Is it really that bad?'

'It is. Not many more energy drains before the whole system starts to bleed to death. We're all three million years too advanced to go back to basking in the sun and expecting to survive. Come and see for yourself if you don't believe me.'

'All right,' sighed Annac. 'But if you want to reach the source of this thing on the other side of the galaxy with my system you're not going to have much success. It's only effective under distances of two hundred light years. Over that it's impossible to select the time the subject matter arrives. It could take ages.'

'Our computer signal doesn't though,' Opu hinted, but Annac remained unconvinced.

The rest of the control staff were not surprised to see Opu and Annac stroll from the balcony to the plans the android engineers had produced.

'We've got enough information to make a transmitter

which will attract the Star Dancer on its own planet. We are going to use its energy imprint to create a signal it'll find difficult to resist. All this will be sent with the components for an android.'

'What's this machine going to look like then?' Opu pointed to the blueprint. 'There's no outer casing,' Annac complained, sensing something aesthetically unpleasant about it.

'Doesn't matter,' Opu told her. 'Will its components transmit on your system?'

'Of course, but not at this range.'

'Good.' Opu smiled beneath her blunt beak. 'If we've ever done anyone any favours in the past, let's hope they were appreciated.' She prepared to open the computer transmission to the watery world of Taigal Rax. 'When we told the Taigalians about our problem they promised to help us.'

'How far away from this Perimeter 84926 are they?'

'One hundred and fifty light years.'

'Then if they transmit it, it'll arrive far too soon, even with compensations for different space time.'

'One of Perimeter 84926's centuries before it actually happens here,' Opu explained, 'This will give the android time to orient itself and be established when the energy source starts developing there . . . I hope.'

'But you'll have no control over the machine,' Annac reminded her. 'We can only transmit it back into their past because we can bisect the time curve Perimeter 84926 has travelled through.'

'Of course we won't have any control over it. The first thing we'll know about it managing to intercept the Star Dancer is when it stops manifesting itself here.'

'And how will that pile of metal and crystal manage to do that?'

'We intend our aquatic friends to take this expensive pile of metal and crystal and build into the plans for the android a sense of what the creatures on Perimeter 84926 look like. It can then change its appearance whenever it needs and even develop living tissue if necessary to move about freely. They can supply it with its power units and any knowledge it needs about the planet, and use your Kybini system to transmit it.'

'Living tissue!' Annac blurted out. The rest of the control staff had frozen at the mention of the word. 'If you're sending something like that back into anyone's time without proper control over it, you'd better pray the Watchers never find out.'

'We will have double checked it, and Taigal Rax will do the same to their additions. It'll only operate its biological processes if they instruct it. Without self-awareness it could hardly do that for itself. We can afford to take the risk because we've got everything to lose if we don't.'

'I believe you,' grunted Annac, unable to think of any more objections. 'So this machine will have already been wandering about on Perimeter 84926 for its last century and will be able to let us know when it has managed to stop the beast that keeps attacking the energy pools?'

'Assuming I start transmitting the information now, just so.' Opu started to feed the programme to Taigal Rax.

'What a way to spend a retirement,' Annac cursed to herself as her old wings fluttered her unsurely home into the pink sunrise.

3

A damp mist rolled across the brooding cliffs fringing the dark sea. Occasional snatches of moonlight lit the very edges of the grey chalk where the breeze from the sea had pushed the mist back, and it glowed like a sinister ribbon. Above the fuming waves an eerie swishing sound echoed at the top of the cliffs, followed by an unlikely tinkling noise as something felt the firmness of the ground beneath it. A couple of seconds passed and another swishing sound was followed by a further tinkling noise. Then another and another, until there was an untidy heap of diamond-metal, crystal, and gold tendons on a cushion of sea thrift and twitch-grass.

As soon as everything had arrived, the glinting components began to arrange themselves, some lifting themselves erect as though trying to peer over the others, and some rolling towards their adjoining members. Each piece knew where it should fit, like mechanical chromosomes, and gradually they assembled themselves into a glittering faceless machine. It sat twinkling in the erratic mist for several moments, checking its components and circuits, then lifted itself erect on two stick-like legs in a crude imitation of a human frame.

Unsurely it picked its way over the unfamiliar ground towards the edge of the cliff. It sent out signals in every direction to make sure of its surroundings, then stood pondering for a few seconds. Without warning, it sprang forward from the cliff and plunged into the dark churning sea below.

There was an onimous rumbling echo from the bowels of the iron-clad ship as its cargo slid across the hold, and tilted it so far over that the deck was partly submerged. The sails and the steam-driven paddles of the merchant ship were useless in the teeth of the storm that was trying to roll it over. The crew was well rehearsed for such a disaster though. They had been expecting something like it for the last eight voyages she had been on. They did not begrudge the owners their insurance money, but they were sure they were not going to be drowned for it. Before the order to abandon ship could be given, the lifeboats were launched and passengers and crew stowed inside them. When someone yelled across the bows to ask whether the inebriated Captain was going down with his ship he sobered up with remarkable speed and slid down the deck to join his first mate in the nearest boat.

'Sheer off! Sheer off!' he was heard to yell. 'Sheer off or we'll all be sucked down with her!' As though that had not already occurred to the sailors battling with oars.

'My cargo! My cargo!' rang out a despairing cry from one of the smaller boats being rowed away from the mêlée towards the cliffs looming out of the spray.

'Better to be alive and have the insurance,' a blond young man hauling at an oar tried to reassure him.

'I don't need your insolence, you young pup!' Mr Humbert retorted.

'Well shut up then you old fool and sit down,' snapped an older woman. 'If you can't help row the boat you might stop rocking it.'

Mr Humbert was obviously not used to being spoken to in such a manner, and would have stood resolutely at the bows glowering if a wave had not thrown him down to the bottom of the boat.

'We're heading straight for the cliffs, Toby!' exclaimed the young woman pulling at the other oar, as she snatched a glance over her shoulder. 'We should have taken a sailor on board with us.'

'You're right, Tasmin,' agreed the young man, feeling a mixture of panic and exhaustion. 'We're just being dragged towards them . . . I'm more used to holding a quill than an oar.'

At that the older woman placed herself between the struggling younger couple and, seizing the end of each oar, tried to add her weight to their efforts. Humbert meanwhile sat facing them, staring stonily at their exertion as though his Victorian affluence had given him some immunity against drowning.

Soon all the other lifeboats with sailors on board were well out of sight and perhaps in safer waters. As much as the three battled with the waves, the cliffs were soon towering above them and sucking the boat towards their stony walls.

'Get down!' yelled the older woman, as one of the oars snapped against the jagged rocks. 'Lie flat . . .'

All four clung to the slats in the bottom of the flooded boat as it banged against one rock after another. At any moment they expected it to disintegrate and pitch them into the swirling water, to be sucked down into its permanent blackness. But suddenly the hammering stopped, and they were being swept into a world of muffled darkness. The roaring torrent was left behind and in its place they could hear the gushing and slurping of water being forced into a large chamber. For a few seconds they were spun round and round, then the boat seemed to travel in a straight line for some distance.

'We're in a tunnel,' the older woman eventually murmured.

'I'm scared, Mrs Angel' whispered Toby. 'Are you all right, Tasmin?'

'I prefer to be in here rather than outside.' Tasmin rose from the bottom of the boat to see if she could catch a glimpse of anything through the pitch blackness. She only succeeded in banging her head on the cave roof.

'Be careful,' said Mrs Angel. 'We could be travelling into a dead end.'

'Then what can we do?' asked Toby.

'It depends on how narrow the passage is. We may be able to wall-walk our way out.'

'You mean like the canal bargees when they come to a tunnel?'

'That's right.'

'Goodness. My legs would never be long enough.'

'You're an inadequate sort of creature aren't you? What made you think you would be a suitable husband for my assistant?'

'Please, Mrs Angel, it's hardly the time and place to discuss that,' remonstrated Tasmin.

'This is the sort of situation which will prove how worthy he really is.'

'But you can't expect Toby to be the one to rescue us. He wasn't even able to save the ledgers he was entrusted with.'

'Then you might have at least considered a more suitable specimen to break your vestal vow for, young lady . . . a ledger clerk indeed.'

'But you can't expect me to keep that vow forever.'

'You will for as long as I employ you. You can hardly expect our class of clientêle to listen to their departed loved ones through the mouth of a housewife or scarlet woman.'

'I'm sure I wouldn't do anything to dishonour Tasmin, Mrs Angel,' protested Toby.

'Fortunately, so am I.'

They would have continued arguing had they not caught sight of an eerily glimmering light ahead of them. They were swept along the jagged passage into a large dimly lit cave. At the far end was a wide platform. The boat came alongside it and nudged to a stop; gratefully they clambered out. Before them the amazed and sodden passengers could see a wall studded with a series of small lights and knobs. Some of the rock was transparent and inside it they could see cavities holding strange machines spinning and clicking in time to some tuneless rhythm.

No one could explain what they had accidentally trans-gressed into, so no one spoke. Gingerly they examined their surroundings, being careful not to touch anything, the thought crossing their minds that they might be trapped there for a long time. Beneath them in the water lapping the platform appeared a glowing sickly light. In it, to their astonishment, they gradually made out a shape walking towards them from the depths. It carried itself like a human being, but its movements were all wrong. As it rose from the water they shrank to the far end of the platform. They were unable to see who their host was because of a long shroud, like a monk's habit, the material of which they noticed was instantly dry as soon as air touched it. Its wearer climbed up some rough steps from the water and emerged on to the platform, cutting off their only chance of escaping in the boat.

'Who are you?' asked Mrs Angel, feeling more than a little daunted by the strange hooded figure.

'Who are *you*?' the figure asked in a metallic clicking voice.

'I am Mrs Angel.' She formally introduced the others in turn as though she were at a dinner party, 'This is Tasmin, and Mr Humbert. And we call this one Toby. He's only a ledger clerk.' She turned back to the figure. 'Now, what is your name?'

'The Kybion,' it replied.

'Rum sort of name,' muttered Toby, but the figure only demanded in reply, 'What are you doing here?'

'Why ask that?' snapped Mrs Angel. 'You must already know.' She was not sure what made her say it.

'You are right, Mrs Angel,' clicked the voice in what might have been surprise. 'You are perceptive.'

'I am a medium.'

The Kybion did not seem to register the meaning of the word, so she explained, 'I can see into the future and contact spirits from the world of the dead.'

As that revelation met with stony silence, Tasmin went on, 'Mrs Angel and I were coming back from France after an important seance when our ship foundered.'

'Wretched iron clads,' snorted Mr Humbert. 'How can anything stay afloat with all that metal rivetted to it?'

'Remember the insurance, Mr Humbert,' Toby dared to

remind him, and received a hefty clip round the ear for his advice.

Before real violence could break out, the Kybion declared abruptly, 'You should all be dead.'

'Probably so,' agreed Mrs Angel. 'But the Good Lord spared us in his infinite mercy.'

'The "Good Lord" had nothing to do with the matter. I made the inlet you were swept into. It was pure chance your boat found it. You should have all been killed on the cliff-face. Things cannot be altered out of time sequence.'

'What do you mean, sir?' demanded Humbert, striding towards the mysterious gowned figure. 'Do you know who I am?'

'You should be dead, Mr Humbert,' was the clinical reply.

At that, Humbert's heavily jowled face glowed red with fury and he reached out to snatch off the concealing hood of the Kybion's habit, saying, 'Now let's see who you are, sir! This mumbo jumbo has gone far enough.'

And so had Mr Humbert. He reeled back in terror at what he saw and toppled from the platform.

The other three looked on in disbelief and horror, ignoring Humbert's calls for help as he splashed about in the shallow water. Standing before them was a faceless jumble of tangled wire tendons and winking crystal arteries. The gown had fallen open to reveal a basic skeleton shape entwined with simulated nerves and supported by semi-transparent muscles. Not even Mrs Angel could think of anything to say to that.

'I am the Kybion,' the alien shape reaffirmed. 'I am not yet whole,' it added in an understatement.

'You're really going to kill us, aren't you?' said Tasmin as Toby wrapped his short arms protectively about her.

'You should have died,' it repeated. 'The fault that you did not is mine.'

'But we don't mind . . . really we don't,' blurted out Toby.

'I am from a future time,' the Kybion went on. 'I cannot interfere with the history of this planet, even to let you live.'

'You are a scoundrel, sir,' spluttered Humbert, dragging

himself on to the platform. 'Not only a scoundrel, but as twisted a piece of machinery as is ever liable to be assembled by a madman.'

'I am not complete.'

'But no one can travel from the future,' snapped Mrs Angel. 'It would be unGodlike if they could.'

'I am the Kybion. I have no gods,' the machine said. 'This god of yours is part of your own longing for the impossible. Many stars away, people can achieve what you call impossible and they do not need gods. I come from them.'

'Why?' asked Tasmin, disengaging herself from Toby to square up to it.

'I was sent to stop a creature they call Vian Solran, Star Dancer, from sucking the life energy of another planet dry,' it replied. 'At some time in the near future it will originate from this world. I am here to wait for it.'

'Why not let us help you instead of killing us?' pleaded Toby. 'What possible harm could we do to the future if you were to let us live?'

The machine hesitated. 'If I were to let you live to help me, I would have to prolong your lives for longer than is natural to your species. Though I could do it, how am I to be sure you would not try to disrupt the future of this world?'

'We could only give you our word,' Tasmin suggested hopefully.

'On this cross,' said Mrs Angel pulling a large crucifix from her blouse.

'Yes, yes,' begged Humbert. 'We couldn't do any more than that.'

Toby was silent. He wanted to live more than anything else, but knew Mrs Angel and Humbert were lying and was not sure whether the Kybion knew it too.

Suddenly, without warning, it reached out a spiked finger and jabbed it in the air towards Toby. 'I will select you. I will give you a longevity process which will double your life span. The others should die.'

'No' Toby found himself protesting against his better

judgement. 'How could you expect me to help you if I know you left the other three to die?' The Kybion had not taken that into consideration, and stood silent for a few seconds. 'At least let them live their natural life spans,' asked Toby.

'No,' said Tasmin. 'You cannot half trust us. We three would know Toby has longevity. There is no reason why we should not be attributed with his integrity.'

The Kybion sensed the deceit in the older woman and man, but was not programmed to take life.

'I won't help you unless Tasmin is able to live for as long as I do,' insisted Toby. 'I don't care how powerful you are. You can't make me help you if I don't want to.' Knowing his mistake before he finished his words, he added, 'And Mrs Angel and Mr Humbert as well.'

'Very well,' it said eventually. 'I will give you all a treatment which will slow your ageing processes down. You will age, but at a much slower rate than is natural. You will not be able to carry on your normal lives. Those who know you must believe you are dead.' Humbert winced at the thought of having to give up his insurance money, but was soon plotting some way round it. 'I will be watching you to make sure you do nothing to harm the future.'

'What is it you want me to do?' Toby inquired, half afraid of the reply he would receive.

'You shall carry a small transmitter which will attract the Star Dancer to you. Its energy pattern was recorded by the planet it threatens. They used this knowledge to design a signal it would find difficult to ignore, whether it was intelligent or not. I was originally going to put the transmitter in a fixed position, but over the passing years the human species could well decide to dig it up or build over it. I cannot carry it because the power in my circuits would interfere with its signal.' The Kybion realised Toby was having severe doubts. 'It will not harm you, and it is unlikely the Star Dancer would. If you do this you may save a whole species of creatures like yourself from extinction.'

'I suppose if I should be dead anyway . . . I've nothing to

lose,' Toby agreed, not knowing which was the better arrangement. 'What will happen when I do meet this "Star Dancer"?'

'Do not worry. I will be here. I will always be here.' It addressed the latter remark to the others. 'You three will carry markers. Ones that will let me know where you are at all times.'

'All right,' said Toby after a pause. 'I'll do it. Where will I carry this trans . . . mitter then? How big is it? What happens when I'm not wearing pockets?'

'You will not need pockets. There are many cavities inside your body into which it will fit quite easily.'

At that, Toby became rigid with fright. The Kybion seemed unaware of what terror any surgical operation held for a Victorian, otherwise it might have explained it would be totally painless.

The others certainly showed no signs of discomfort when it gave them their longevity treatment. It seemed to consist of nothing more than impregnating the skin with a series of needles in the shape of a brush. A quick application to each and it was over, but to Toby it felt as though it took hours. The machine may have been incomplete, but it had sense enough not to let the three realise how it had fitted the signalling devices that would let it know where they were from now on. Each marker was minute and would cling to their skeletons for as long as they lived.

The Kybion then produced clothes from one of the cavities behind the chamber's walls, and Tasmin, Mrs Angel and Humbert were completely recostumed. They were given generous amounts of money, sufficient to allow them to idle their time away in luxury if they wished.

'Well Toby, perhaps we might meet again,' Tasmin said.

Even that affectionate reassurance could not revive Toby's good humour though.

'Take care of him,' Mrs Angel told the Kybion imperiously, having to acknowledge that the ledger clerk had saved their lives. 'Remember his intelligence is no more than matches his station.'

Sensing it was unsure what her employer meant, Tasmin added, 'Don't hurt him.'

'Let us out of here,' Mr Humbert demanded impatiently.

Toby found the presence of mind to give Tasmin a self-conscious hug, but they were quickly parted by Mrs Angel.

'Remember your vow, my girl,' she chided.

'There is a tunnel running under these cliffs which leads to the nearest town,' said the Kybion. 'Remember, wherever you go, I will always know.'

With that warning ringing in their ears they hastened away to freedom.

Not appearing too concerned whether they reached the other end of the dimly lit tunnel or not, the Kybion returned to the trembling Toby who wished he had gone with them. The ledger clerk could not believe what was happening to him. The more he thought about it, the more his senses became numbed, until the clammy air and sight of the robot made him faint away where he stood.

4

Gabrielle sighed a deep breath of relief when she saw the ugly brick and cement receding behind her and the train began to travel through velvet-green fields rippling with new corn. The June landscape had already made her feel better than she had for the past few weeks. She was glad she had resisted the temptation to take a high-speed train to the other end of the country for bright lights and candyfloss company, because here she was able to see things in more detail. She did not want to dash anywhere, just have time to unwind.

Gabrielle knew in her own mind she had passed every A-level she had sat over the last two months, and would probably not have worried too much if she hadn't. Not many orphans had such an assured future as she. Not many children grew up with the intelligence she possessed. Perhaps that was why she was so restless, yet tired.

She was a strong healthy girl, and showed no sign of the severe injuries she had received in the car crash which had killed her Indian parents when she was four. No next of kin could be found, but she did not regret being put into a children's home. They had been very indulgent with her, and her foster parents over the past nine years more so. She had never been an easy child, but something told those caring for her that she was exceptional. Far from pretty, her looks were none the less striking. Her expression was thoughtful, as if she were always pondering something. Which was probably true. Her eyes were large, dark and intelligent enough to belong to a woman twice her age.

As she walked down the sloping path that led to Smuggler's Row, the small terrace of cottages where her foster father's sister lived, Gabrielle watched the swifts and seagulls circle over the clifftops. The air was better here than anywhere else

she could remember. If it were not for the railway station it would probably have been too isolated for people to live there at all.

Gabrielle was fond of her foster aunt Penny and Penny's ten-year-old daughter Paula, and almost regretted that they would be taking a morning train to go on a holiday of their own. Everyone she knew thought she had been mad to want to travel to this remote spot and live in her aunt's cottage without company for over three weeks. She had never seen the place before, but somehow it seemed just what she wanted.

'It *is* remote here,' Penny told her as she poured the tea with one hand and rapped Paula's knuckles with the other as she tried to sneak another piece of fruit cake. 'But with the train and the occasional bus you can get almost anywhere. Even walk to the village if you want. It's not a mile up the road.'

'I just want to rest.' sighed Gabrielle, 'Doing all the things adolescent girls should do must be tiring enough, but trying to *avoid* doing all the things adolescent girls are expected to do is even more tiring.'

'Don't waste your life away,' Penny smiled. 'You'll soon be old enough.' She herself was in her forties, and still attractive.

'Is there a library in the village?' Gabrielle asked suddenly, as though remembering something of great importance.

'A small one, but there's a main one in the town. I've got tickets for both.' Penny went to her handbag and pulled three tickets from her purse. 'One is Paula's, but you might as well keep them all together.' She handed them to Gabrielle.

'Thanks a lot. I might as well take a walk into the village tomorrow.'

'Good idea. We'll have to be off early, so you'll have the whole of the day to yourself.'

Gabrielle spent that night in fitful sleep. She was visited by the turbulent dreams that had haunted her for as long as she could remember. Recently they had become worse with the

exams, but she was hoping they would subside with some peace and quiet. She woke the next morning feeling as though every fibre in her body needed more than peace and quiet if they were ever to untangle themselves.

Gabrielle saw Penny and Paula on to the train, then returned to the cottage to sort out a pair of stout walking shoes from her suitcase.

It was threatening rain, but there was hardly any wind as she strode out over the glistening shingle, untouched by holidaymakers' feet. Growing tired of walking on the pebbles she climbed the crumbling steps braced by railway sleepers and continued along the top of the cliffs. The only other people she saw were a plump woman letting her dog exercise her, and the motionless figure of a fair-haired man watching her from a distance.

'Who is that?' she asked the plump dog owner in passing, for something to say.

'No idea, but he's always out here watching for something,' beamed the woman. 'It's about time he found what he was looking for after all these years.'

Later, in the village library, Gabrielle found a volume to satisfy her appetite. It was in good condition though published many years ago and the librarian slipped her a glance of admiration as she took it out.

Her striking looks and billowing black hair soon caught the attention of the small community. An Indian girl in mackintosh and walking brogues must have been something of a novelty in those parts. Curious to know more about her, some people went out of their way to be friendly, though others kept their distance. Not wanting to appear stand-offish, though it was her natural inclination, Gabrielle managed to supply them with enough information about herself to satisfy their immediate curiosity and, not wanting to appear uninterested in their small world, enquired about the man who stood on top of the cliff. The two old women with whom she struck up a conversation smiled secretly, and put her ignorance down to youth.

'He's been looking out for goodness knows what on top of them cliffs for as long as I can remember,' one of them said. 'And I'm seventy.'

'He doesn't look a day over forty-five though,' joined in the other. 'And I think my old father said he could remember him too.'

'Mind you, Dot,' the other woman reminded her, 'your old dad's brain did go eventually. My Ma reckoned it was his father he saw.'

'Might have been, but I don't remember his funeral. I've been to the funeral of everyone who died around here, and I can't remember him ever dying.'

Whatever the vagaries of the two old ladies' memories, Gabrielle had to admit that her curiosity had been fired. The man had not looked very old from where she was standing, and she was curious to know how a possible seventy year old could look no more than forty-five. She could picture him watching on the cliff above the village as she stood chatting, and inquired, 'Why doesn't somebody ask him?'

The two old ladies were silent for a moment,

'It probably hasn't occurred to them,' Dot replied.

'He never gets near enough to anyone to let them,' her companion rejoined. 'Even his groceries are put on his back doorstep where he leaves a cheque and list for the next week.'

'You going to ask him then, dear?' Dot inquired, half in humour and half in hope.

'I could do.'

'He'll run off before you can, but I wouldn't stop you trying. A sturdy girl like you could probably catch him.' And at that the two women fell about cackling.

Gabrielle took the opportunity of their mirth to escape, and made her way to the top of the cliff where she hoped her quarry still stood. She felt compelled to speak to the strange figure. Even from fifty yards away she could feel his pale grey eyes observing her determined approach. He did not run off as the old women had suggested, but remained stock still.

27

As she came closer, Gabrielle could sense the coldness of the man's penetrating gaze. His hair was fair, nearly white, and his skin had almost the pallor of death, but it was difficult to believe his face belonged to a man of forty-five, let alone seventy. His features seemed to have no lines of experience, and a polo-necked sweater concealed his neck where tell-tale signs of age could usually be found.

'Good morning,' Gabrielle said cheerfully.

The expression in the pale eyes became suspicious, if not hostile. 'Go away,' the man said.

As he spoke Gabrielle sensed the depth of his frosty personality and remarked, in spite of herself, 'Why, you're not that old at all.'

'Go away,' he repeated. He turned on his heel and almost ran from the edge of the cliff towards a flat-roofed bungalow nestling in a gully.

That should have been enough to convince Gabrielle he did not want to hold any conversation. But there was something so magnetic and mysterious about the stranger that she could not resist following him down the slope. He stood in the porch of the bungalow watching her, and before she got too close and scared him inside, she called out 'What's the matter? I didn't mean to alarm you.'

'You didn't. Who sent you?' Encouraged by the odd question, Gabrielle walked down to him.

'Why, nobody. I was only trying to be sociable.'

'No one round here tries to be sociable with me,' he retorted flatly. 'Are you sure no one sent you?'

'Of course not. I only arrived here yesterday. Why should anyone have sent me?'

He did not reply, just gave her a cool, hard, penetrating look.

'The truth is,' Gabrielle admitted, 'two old ladies in the village were trying to kid me you were seventy, and I didn't believe them.'

'You are right, I am not seventy.'

'I can see that now. Don't you let anyone talk to you?'

'Not if I can avoid it,' the man murmured through tight lips. 'You aren't English?'

'Yes, I am. My parents were Indian, but I was born here. I can't remember them though. I was brought up in a children's home. I couldn't even pronounce my own name if you were to ask me.'

'What are you called instead then?'

'Gabrielle. What's your name?'

'Never you mind,' he said firmly enough for her not to ask again.

'You're an odd sort of person.' Gabrielle was quite unable to make him out. 'I'll leave you alone if that's what you want.'

The man said nothing. He could see that his frosty manner did not intimidate the eighteen-year-old as it had older people. As she walked back to the cliff, his gaze followed her with a mixture of fascination and suspicion.

5

That night sleep came quickly to Gabrielle, and without any dreams bad enough to disturb her. The next morning she woke early. It was already light, and she looked out at the gulls circling in the refreshing sea air, at the same time drowsily allowing random thoughts to flow through her mind.

Still half asleep, Gabrielle seemed to see the ghostly figure of a young man standing by the window of the bedroom. He was not very large and had a friendly mobile expression but, strangest of all, he was wearing clothes of the nineteenth-century. His frock coat and trousers were almost threadbare and the chisel-toed shoes had all but lost their original shape. By comparison, his frilled cream shirt, which was set off by a faded maroon velvet waistcoat, looked quite expensive. He was hatless and his beaming face seemed to sit on a wide cravat tied with meticulous care.

Gabrielle lay watching him, wondering what part of her fancy had conjured him up, when he began to pull a newspaper from under his arm. As he unfurled it she could see that it was called *The Daily Bugle* and when he held it out towards her she could also make out the date. There must have been something peculiar about it. Though he was obviously Victorian, the date of the paper was 1 April 1917. At that she realised her mind must have been playing practical jokes on her. With a grunt of disgust she woke herself up and sat upright to make sure she had been dreaming.

All through breakfast Gabrielle could not help smiling to herself about the unlikely visitor and his wrongly dated newspaper, but started to wonder whether such a thing as *The Daily Bugle* ever existed. Then, as she idly sorted out some clothes to wear, a forceful urge to go to the town library and

find out struck her. There was a bus in fifteen minutes. She finished dressing and dashed out, combing her long hair on the way to the bus stop.

She told herself she was mad to travel eight miles on a silly whim like this; but the buses were very infrequent, and the trains did not pass through the town, so she would have had to fight back her curiosity for hours before another opportunity arrived.

From the market square Gabrielle went straight to the main library without consulting the map. She had been given specific directions to every place of importance by her fellow bus passengers, who were only too glad somebody should be interested in exploring the nooks and crannies of their corner of the world. The area had never been a great tourist attraction. It somehow lacked the places of amusement and synthetic splendour other towns possessed. Even the library was still housed in its Victorian monument dedicated to the education of the lower orders, and was permeated with disinfectant and the austere silence due it. Gabrielle could feel her muscles tense as she noticed for the first time that her new shoes squeaked.

Being able to ask for a specific paper with an exact date meant the librarian did not have to ask her embarrassing questions about what she was looking for. Which was just as well, because she was not sure herself. Gabrielle was amazed to know there was once a local paper called *The Daily Bugle,* and not only that, but it had not yet been stored in the vaults of the town hall, also Victorian and filled to capacity with files, rate demands and staff.

1 April 1917 was apparently a Sunday, so she was brought the next day's edition. Something at the back of her mind told Gabrielle she would never have remembered a date as ordinary as 2 April, and she sensed some uncanny reasoning in the apparition. The news-sheet in its perspex cover was placed in her hands, and she could feel them shaking as she took it. This was getting too eerie, even for her. She thanked the librarian and carried it to a stand where she carefully

turned the discoloured pages, scouring every last detail.

As she came to page five, Gabrielle was unable to believe her eyes. She gave a slight gasp. The man reading opposite glanced up to give her a concerned look. Under the heading of 'Man proves he is sixty-seven years old. Court upholds decision he is not eligible for conscription', was a picture of a man who could not have been over twenty-five. Yet it was, without doubt, the face of the man she had met on the cliffs. His name was Alfred Tobias Wendle.

Still stunned at the discovery, Gabrielle quickly glanced through the rest of the paper. She had a rational, thorough mind and would have cursed herself for having missed something in the moment of revelation. Then she took the paper to the photocopier to make a record of the front cover and the article. Not without some difficulty, though, as the machine swallowed four coins before printing anything reasonably like the original. Gabrielle put its malfunctioning down to the fact it must have been Victorian as well and did not bother to ask for her money to be refunded. She was in too much of a hurry to grieve over forty pence.

As the bus carried her home she tried to think of a rational explanation for the picture. As the old woman had suggested, it could have been the man's father. But she doubted it. A face like his was too distinctive to have been inherited so exactly. There was only one thing for it. She must confront him again. After yesterday's encounter it might not be a very promising idea, but it was the only one she had.

As Gabrielle changed into her walking brogues she tried to sort out the relevance of the young Victorian man who had presented the paper to her, but could not think what connection he had with the matter apart from blending with the town's architecture.

When she reached the clifftop where the man had been standing the day before, he was nowhere to be seen, so she went down to the bungalow and knocked resolutely on the door, half expecting a bucket of water to be tipped over her head from the flat roof. But to her amazement, a voice from

inside called out, 'Come in, the door is open.'

It was his voice all right. Cool, without any trace of cordiality. She went inside, through a small hall, and into a large room. Everything was immaculately tidy, even the figure in the polo-neck sweater sitting at the table over a mug of coffee was groomed like a schoolmaster supervising an exam.

'Do you take sugar in coffee?' he asked efficiently.

Gabrielle nodded and he added a large spoonful to another steaming mug. 'You can come in and sit down if you like. Standing around like that looks untidy.'

'You like everything tidy?'

'I have a very tidy mind.'

Gabrielle slumped carelessly into the chair facing him, clutching the photocopies she had taken that morning. She looked into his cool grey eyes and asked, 'How old are you?'

'One hundred and twenty-seven,' he replied without blinking, not moving his gaze and making sure he did not miss her reaction.

'You've worn well.' She half believed him.

'It's not a blessing.' He paused. 'How much are you capable of believing?'

'How much do you want to tell me?'

'I cannot tell you part of the truth. I must tell you everything. I am not good at talking to other people. It is unlikely anything I have to say would be believed.'

'People in the village believe there is something strange about you. Why not confirm their suspicions?'

'Because people will only believe what they have been taught is possible. What is out of their experience becomes impossible.'

'I was going to ask you about this.' Gabrielle put the photocopies on the table. 'But you seem to have anticipated it.'

'I was a young man once,' he said. 'Quite a lively good-natured fellow in a naive way. I was a ledger clerk and lived in near poverty. I wore the same suit and shoes for years. The

only new garment I was able to afford for a long while was a frilled cream-coloured shirt.'

'But that young man whom I saw this morning couldn't have been you ?' Gabrielle protested. 'He hardly bore any resemblance to you. He was fair and the same height . . . but his expression was so different.'

'An expression can change over a century, even if the face doesn't.'

'What was his name?'

'He was called Toby.'

'Alfred Tobias Wendle?'

'Yes.'

'Then you are Toby.'

'No,' he said sharply. 'Don't call me that.' He rose abruptly to go to the window as if to escape her.

'Why did you want me to know about you after you've kept everything to yourself for so long?' Gabrielle enquired carefully.

'Because you may be intelligent enough to believe me,' Wendle replied with his back to her.

'And?' prompted Gabrielle.

'Now there is a problem. I believe I could carry on growing old at this slow rate if I can't find someone to help me,' Wendle turned and saw her puzzled expression. 'Longevity is not the marvellous thing it is made out to be by those who have never known it. It is a living death. After so many years, even your brain cells do not age, but they become tired of the same old thoughts and same old tasks. Although they do not die, they do not grow either. Nature designed the human mind to have only a certain span. You have to sleep for days at a time to escape the boredom of it, and when you have to do that your real self must escape from the body for fear of it going mad.'

'I see. But why aren't you able to age at the same pace as everyone else?'

Wendle returned to the table and sat facing her again. Before starting his story, he gave her one last long look as

34

though to reassure himself he was not making a mistake.

'I gave my word I would never tell this to a living soul, but I believe the other party concerned has broken its pledge,' he explained. 'If I am right, I must tell someone.'

Gabrielle listened to his extraordinary tale in silence but internally she was finding it very difficult to take. A planet on the other side of the galaxy, an energy vampire called Vian Solran, Star Dancer, and a faceless robot capable of doubling human life spans . . . It was obvious Wendle was no practical joker, though. Both fascinated and alienated by him at the same time, Gabrielle was totally convinced of his integrity. Behind his brittle exterior there was a vulnerable creature she was willing to help. Perhaps the greatest assistance she could provide, though, was not to think him mad. Gabrielle made the necessary mental leap and decided to believe him.

'Everything seems to be going wrong now,' Wendle said.

'Why?' asked Gabrielle.

'The other three, Tasmin, Humbert and Mrs Angel contacted me recently. They have somehow managed to remove the markers the Kybion had given them to keep track of their movements. After doing this they were able to amass fortunes, Mr Humbert by collecting ship insurances and Mrs Angel and Tasmin by using powers they had developed over the years to set themselves up as mediums again. They were not content with the fortunes they had though. They knew I was being used to attract an energy source of immense power, and what could be more profitable nowadays than energy?'

'But if you don't know what form it's liable to arrive in, how on earth will they manage to control it?'

'Greed can make people blind to the most obvious things. I am not afraid of losing my life, but I am afraid of what they might try and do with this Star Dancer were they to meet it.'

'But if a highly advanced race on another planet can't control it, how could they hope to ?' Gabrielle asked again in disbelief.

'They couldn't. They will probably take away the chance of

the Kybion intercepting it and let it loose on this planet as well.'

'Then the Kybion must be warned.'

'If I knew where to find it, it would be. It should have contacted me a long while ago when the Star Dancer was due to arrive, but I haven't seen either of them. That's why I'm afraid of being left like this, and even more afraid of what could happen to this other planet. I have only one advantage.'

'What's that?'

'You believe me. Even if you aren't able to help me find the Kybion, now everything is going wrong, it's a relief someone else knows.'

Gabrielle pondered for a few moments, then had to ask, 'Why don't the other three have the same problem with longevity as you do?'

'Because they have materialistic minds and are now able to move about as much as they want. If I were to travel from this area, the transmitter might encounter some interference that would stop it functioning.'

'Perhaps that's what's happened already, and that's why the Kybion hasn't been able to contact you.'

'The Kybion was incomplete when I first met it, but should have managed to overcome that problem after all this time. And I would feel it if the transmitter stopped,' Wendle said. 'If Humbert or the other two were to try and move me from this place, that is what might happen.'

'At least they wouldn't get the Star Dancer.' She could see he was not impressed. 'Yes. I suppose that could be pretty disastrous as well.'

'Especially if they tried to cut the transmitter out of me. At least, I wouldn't be very happy about it.'

'Don't suppose the police would be any use?' Wendle gave her an even cooler look. 'No, they wouldn't believe even part of it. There's only one thing for it then,'

'What's that?'

'Toby will have to let me know if anything happens to you.'

'No!' Wendle snapped.

'Why not? The other three aren't able to use their spirit forms in the same way and find out what we're up to, are they?'

'Not as far as I know. But I did not intend you to take any risks.'

'Who says I will ?' Gabrielle replied innocently.

Wendle paused for a moment, then seemed satisfied. He poured out two more mugs of coffee. They sat in silence drinking them until the grandfather clock, looking oddly out of place in the uncluttered room, struck the hour with a resounding hollow chime. It seemed to urge Gabrielle to move, and obediently she gathered up the photocopies and her shoulder bag and left.

That night Gabrielle slept unusually deeply. It was as though the revelations of the day had been too much for her consciousness to digest and it was taking what relief it could before another strange day arrived.

Wendle sat awake at the table in his bungalow, too cautious to fall asleep, though his body craved rest. The breeze seemed to catch the kitchen window and blow it open but he was too tired to go and close it. If he had been his usual vigilant self he would have sensed the figure standing behind him and been able to duck out of the way of the quick hand which pressed a pad over his nose and mouth. After a brief violent struggle, all the cool breezes of the Channel could not have roused him.

6

With a sharp crack, the screen measuring the level in the energy pool shattered. Opu did not even turn to look at it. She was too busy concentrating on keeping the power as constant as she could. It was either that or shutting down another refractor completely, and with five others out of commission that would have been disastrous. Everyone's consumption had already been rationed and the energy-giving yellow sun was about to enter its short phase. By the time it was at its regular meridian again it could well be shining down on a world minus intelligent life.

'Damn evolution,' swore Opu. 'Why the heck did we need continuous nourishment?'

'Can't invent anything to shift us back in time,' a familiar voice told her from the balcony.

'Come inside, Annac. You might as well be in here as anywhere else when we all drop out like spent meteors, one by one round the globe.'

'Not working, eh?' Annac joined the harassed controller. 'You invented it. What could have gone wrong?'

'Did it arrive there?'

'So Taigal Rax says.'

'Then my end went all right. Must have been your machine or the fancy bits they added to it.'

'But it must have worked,' insisted Opu. 'It was faultless. We checked it time and again.'

'Has it contacted them?' asked Annac.

'Not yet. They can't raise it.'

'Then they must have built a mind of its own into it. After all, we don't know enough about these creatures to anticipate what idiosyncrasies it was essential to give it.'

'It may have made a mistake.'

'You mustn't let it cross your mind.'

'The thought has been trampling through my mind ever since we should have been receiving results.'

'You need a short break.'

'You must be joking.'

'Believe me,' said Annac, 'I did a permanent shift when there were those solar flares which surged and shattered eleven refractors, and if I hadn't taken a short break I would never have thought my way out of it. Don't worry, the problem will still be here when you come back. You could go and see your youngster if you want.'

'*That* I would not survive at the present time.'

'If you don't change your mind about that child soon it could grow up with a complex.'

'If that bundle of circuits and crystals doesn't do something about this Star Dancer soon, nobody will have the chance to grow up.'

'Still, I want you to meet someone.'

'Oh?'

'It's not far. Looks as though the creature is through with you for this shift anyway.' She pointed to the remains of the energy level.

Opu saw that it was still and sighed with relief. She handed over to one of the other station staff and went to the balcony with Annac.

'Where to ?' Opu asked.

'Just follow me,' Annac told her.

'Well, don't swerve about, will you. My reflexes aren't up to avoiding too many mid-air collisions.'

'My wings are as steady as they ever were,' Annac assured her with the arrogance of old age, and lurched from the balcony into the air.

Many near collisions later, Annac and Opu were circling over the untidy clutter of spherical homes stacked higgledy-piggledy on top of each other over thousands of years. They looked an eyesore from the air, but some of them were so old no one bothered to pull them down. They thought it was only

a matter of time before they fell down of their own accord. Annac spiralled towards one of the lowest in the stack and Opu followed at a safe distance. Alighting on a narrow balcony and passing through a curtain of light beams they found themselves in a large round room littered with antique apparatus.

'Hey,' shouted Annac to a recess in the room, 'Don't you know there's an emergency on?'

'Then how did you manage to find the time to come here?' came back a voice. 'I always thought you were so invaluable, unlike us poor seers.'

'Because I've come to consult a seer,' Annac shouted back, and in so doing woke a lounging figure which rolled over onto its back, crumpling a wing.

'What a way to spend an emergency,' she commented.

'I was trying to conserve energy until you lit in here like a miracle from the moon,' retorted the recumbent figure. 'I am very energy conscious at the moment.'

'Aren't we all,' agreed Opu wryly.

'Come on Anaru,' called Annac. 'We haven't got all this sun. It was your idea after all.'

'I've just finished setting it up,' Anaru flitted from the alcove. She immediately threw her arms about Opu in greeting and completely ignored Annac, 'I'm sure it might help if we give it a chance,' she bubbled. 'Now everyone clear the loop please.' She ushered the reclining body out. 'We need all the room we can get for this.'

'But this is an old-fashioned mental loop,' said Opu as soon as she recognised the equipment.

'That's right, that's right,' said Anaru fluttering her wings in excitement. 'And you'll never guess who I got through to only a short while ago?'

'Who?' asked Opu, just managing to be polite.

'The Water Planet.'

'She means Taigal Rax,' Annac prompted, though Opu had already guessed.

'We are already able to contact them at the speed of thought,' Opu reminded her.

'Ah . . .' said Anaru lifting a stubby finger, 'But are you able to contact the planet where the Kybion is?'

'Of course not. It would take the Kybion longer than it has to build a receiver, and by the time it had finished it would be more than a little conspicuous. At the moment the wretched thing won't even contact Taigal Rax.'

'But what if you *could* contact it?'

'The Kybion is a machine. It does not have a spirit you can raise.'

'But humans have!'

'Oh no . . . I've got all the problems I need for one life time.'

'Why not?' asked Annac, who had not been known, in her youth, for flights of fancy.

'This is an evolving species. Even if we could contact the humans, it is very unlikely they would understand us.'

'We're still evolving. Any species that isn't is an extinct one. And it's unlikely that all these humans are that aggressive.'

'How do you make the selection from this distance?'

'If we make a mistake we can easily break off,' Anaru reminded her. 'We only have to shut down the power. Let me show you how it works.' Opu lowered her beak in disapproval. 'Please . . .'

'Oh, all right,' Opu said somewhat disagreeably, and Anaru was already connecting the equipment before the words were out of her mouth.

'I'll just let them know I'm coming through.' She dashed into the alcove.

'Hey,' called Opu, 'That's cheating. How did she manage to get a link into the computer signal?' she said to Annac.

'Stop complaining. It doesn't make any difference to your transmission.'

'Get on with it then.' Opu snapped at Anaru as she reappeared.

'Now don't rush me,' Anaru protested. 'I must concentrate.' She sat upright on the floor with her wings outspread, looking like an ancient statuette. 'Don't interrupt, and look at the screen.'

Annac and Opu joined her on the floor and did as she said.

With a beam of power playing about her broad skull, Anaru's thoughts were projected on to the frequency selected on the screen. Within seconds, an image began to flicker before them and soon they saw the distinct outline of one of their aquatic friends.

'You can speak to her if you become part of the loop,' Anaru's thoughts told Opu over the transmitter. 'There'll be no language problem as long as you do not move out of it.'

Somewhat impressed by Anaru's achievement, Opu moved into the loop and carefully studied the amphibious features on the screen. They were shimmering silver and framed in white-edged scales. Double lids protected the eyes, and a nostril in the centre of the forehead occasionally opened and closed.

'My name is Controller Opu,' she thought into the transmitter and the reply came back immediately.

'I am Healphani-Kioyono. I know of you, but am not connected with the transmission of the Kybion. We hope your problem is resolved soon.'

'So do I,' Opu absently thought, and it was immediately transmitted across the galaxy.

'Anaru told us she would like to link with the planet Perimeter 84926. If you are willing, we can supply Anaru with our co-ordinates of the Kybion, and see if she can pick up a human sensitive in its vicinity?'

'As long as it doesn't interfere with its function, you can do as you wish.' Opu was becoming more and more impressed by the minute. 'But I will be making my contacts over the computer signal.'

'Of course. This is purely something experimental, but we could boost Anaru's signal through our equipment should she need it. We naturally would not want the Kybion to fail, and

42

we will help you try anything you feel necessary.'

'We must conserve the power now, Healphani,' Anaru cut in. 'Many thanks. I'll be back to you as soon as we have a locator set up here,' and she slapped the disc which shut down the power to the equipment.

'Well?' said Annac, knowing Opu had changed her mind since she had come in.

'Yes,' admitted Opu. 'You're not often wrong.' Then added as an afterthought, 'But even if you can reach someone on that planet, how will you make them understand, let alone help us?'

'We can talk through thoughts so we won't need a translator.'

'It's purely a matter of selecting the right human sensitive,' explained Anaru.

'Forgive me,' Opu said, 'but it is my job to be cynical. I am not handed prizes for believing in miracles.'

'I'm not surprised you had a brat for a child,' Annac said drily. 'I'll see you later Anaru.' She rose.

'Well, don't come back here and interfere until I tell you,' Anaru warned as she fidgeted herself out of her statuesque position. 'Your ideas have too many angles to be of any use in here. Goodbye, Opu. I hope we see each other again.'

'You're the seer. You should know whether that's ever likely to happen,' Opu reminded her somewhat unkindly, but Anaru just chuckled and returned to her alcove.

7

It was again about dawn when Gabrielle half woke and turned to see the now familiar figure of Toby standing by the window. He was holding something in his hand. It looked like an address written on a sheet of paper. She compelled herself to read it, although she was not aware of its significance. With the pencil and paper she had placed beside her bed the night before Gabrielle managed to copy the words before he faded from her sight.

As she shook herself awake, she realised that his expression had been tense and unsmiling. Remembering her conversation with Wendle she knew something was wrong. She tumbled out of bed to go to the bathroom and splash water on her face. Then she returned to the bedroom to read the address she had written on the pad. 'High Acre Grange, Haymaker's Green' it read. Wondering whether her mind was playing tricks again she went to the map and actually found a place called Haymaker's Green. Gabrielle had no idea what to do next.

She assumed Wendle had been captured and taken to that address. Even if she told the police, no one there would be likely to admit it and let them search the Grange without something better than her suspicion to go on, and the address was a good twelve miles across country. Then she remembered Penny's bike in the backyard. It stood under a primitive lean-to shed, and fortunately was not padlocked. She snatched a quick breakfast and a shower, then dressed in corduroys and shirt, trying to look as inconspicuous as possible. Armed with map and address she peddled furiously along the narrow path to Wendle's bungalow.

When she arrived the door was ajar, and when she entered it was obvious by the mess that he had left in something of a

hurry, without having time to tidy up. In fact it looked as though one almighty struggle had taken place. Back on to the bike she jumped after working out the quickest route to Haymaker's Green.

Even Gabrielle felt the pain of cycling non-stop for those twelve miles and when she had finished circling round the wide green to find the right address, the sight of the long drive leading to the house nearly filled her with despair. And what was she going to do when she did reach the door? The only thing she could think of was to apply for a job as a scullery maid. The place looked as though it needed a staff of hundreds to keep it going. Having the sense not to go to the huge front door at the top of two flights of wide steps, she quickly sorted out where the tradesman's entrance was and made for that over a courtyard of pale pink gravel chips.

Before she could dismount, her path was crossed by a tall black man who looked as though he must have been in charge of something.

'Hello there,' she sang out. 'Friend of mine says you need someone to work in the kitchen.'

The man's features were immobile for a moment as though rapid thoughts were passing behind them, then his face lit up.

'No, no — she meant a laundry maid.'

'Oh . . .' Gabrielle was glad it was a cleaner job. 'Got no references.'

'That's all right. Nobody stops here long anyway. You probably won't either. When can you start?'

'Now if you want,' she told him, trying not to sound too enthusiastic and make him suspicious.

'You're a big girl. Uniform probably won't fit you . . . but nobody will notice. Still, I can show you the way about today. Got your number?'

'Number?' Gabrielle queried with convincing slowness.

'Yes, young lady. Insurance number.' He was obviously used to the problem. 'We have to pay so you can get tranquillisers on the National Health after you've been working here for a couple of days.' He saw her blank

expression. 'Oh, don't worry, I'll show you how to apply for it. Stow your bike over there and come inside.' He bounced into the staff entrance.

Even the servants' working area was impressive, and in the subdued light Gabrielle's escort looked even more imposing, or would have done if it were not for that nonchalant bounce in his step. As he passed the occasional maid, secretary or thinly disguised guard, he greeted them all in the same way, with a quick insincere grin and flourish of the hand. By the time Gabrielle had been shown all the rooms she needed to know about, she seriously began to wonder how anybody, even a crook, could have managed to employ this unlikely, irreverent person as a butler. Then finally she was shown to a large bedroom with curtained bed, wall tapestries and marble fireplace.

'Linen in this place will have to be changed every day,' remarked her escort. 'Got a special visitor coming tomorrow. Be your first job.'

'Oh? Must be a fussy sort of geezer,' she said, not looking forward to the task.

'Well, I suppose surgeons are.'

Gabrielle managed to gulp down an exclamation of horror and said instead, 'What's your name then?'

'Weatherby,' was the reply.' 'What's yours?'

'Jennifer,' she answered quickly.

Weatherby looked disapprovingly down at her faded corduroys, checked shirt and tangled hair, and said slowly, 'No . . . You couldn't be a Jennifer.'

'No?' Gabrielle felt a cold sweat round her neck.

'Scheherazade,' he decided. 'Old man'll like that better. Might even suit you when you're tidied up.'

'Oh . . .' Gabrielle sighed with relief, hoping she would not have to know a thousand and one tales as well. 'When do I have to start in the morning then?'

'Eight thirty.' Gabrielle could not help grimacing. 'Or whenever you like. Could live in if you want. Can't be too fussy in this place. As long as things get done we aren't

bothered by anyone. It's his heavy boys Mr Gunn keeps tabs on.'

'Heavy boys?' Gabrielle exclaimed.

'We have trouble with the mice,' grinned Weatherby cynically, 'They won't bother you. He keeps them on short leads.'

As Gabrielle followed Weatherby back down the stairs and tried to keep track of where she was, she asked rather tentatively,

'Don't suppose there's any chance of stopping here tonight is there?' Weatherby threw a blithe quizzical look back over his shoulder at her. 'Only I got trouble at home y'see.'

'Ah. No problem, if that's what you want. You'll have to get your own meal today though if you want to eat. The cook's going through one of her tricky phases. Mr Gunn's been playing her up something awful and she's a bit sensitive at the moment.'

'Oh thanks. And I don't mind where I sleep.' But Weatherby had bounced too far ahead of her to hear.

In the large basement kitchen Gabrielle was introduced to the sensitive cook. The delicate frills of her blouse sleeves and collar beneath the white overall, and the heavy mesh stockings, clung awkwardly to the contours of a very solid-boned frame.

'Call me Alice,' the cook said in a husky voice, reaching out to take Gabrielle's hand.

'Her real name's Arthur, but call her Alice,' Weatherby explained, despite a warning glance from the cook.

'Don't pay any attention to him, my dear. Because this place finds it difficult to keep staff it attracts all sorts of riff raff. Though it's not surprising. You've no idea what a dreadful man Mr Gunn can be.'

'That's right,' said Weatherby, 'Go and put her off.'

'It wouldn't hurt you to do the laundry once in a while. You always seem to be interfering in everyone else's jobs.'

'I'm paid to. I am the head butler after all.'

'Head butler indeed,' sneered Alice. 'You're the only

butler who's ever been here since you rolled up three months ago.'

'Four.'

'Is Mr Gunn really that bad?' interrupted Gabrielle before Alice could get really worked up.

'Only if you meet him,' Weatherby said reassuringly.

'I won't need to, will I?'

'Oh, you shouldn't worry,' Alice told her. 'He'll like a handsome young thing like you. Only don't go and make the mistake of throwing up the first time you set eyes on his face.'

Gabrielle's eyebrows must have risen sufficiently to prompt Weatherby to explain, 'Mr Gunn's facial attributes are not all that attractive.'

'He's grotesque,' stated Alice.

This certainly sounded like the Mr Humbert Wendle had described to Gabrielle, and the house and guards were easily capable of concealing a prisoner without anyone else knowing.

Gabrielle only met three other maids, a handyman, two gardeners and a kitchen maid, and wondered how they managed to maintain the place by themselves, but she discovered that Mr Gunn's bodyguards were the only ones allowed near him to do anything he needed. He seemed to manage his eccentric roost with the grip of a Victorian patriarch.

An older woman and her companion were the only other people to visit the place that day, and they stayed no more than an hour. Managing to busy herself convincingly by running backwards and forwards along the long landing which overlooked the comings and goings in the main hall, Gabrielle whiled away her first day carrying bundles of laundry. Most of it went into the huge washing machines, and anything that needed ironing was done by one of the maids.

Although she was quite exhausted by the evening, she had noticed the much used door beneath the stairs opening and closing automatically to let the well-groomed heads of guards pass through. Because she could only see the tops of heads

from the landing, one of them might have been Mr Gunn for all she knew. Gabrielle had better sense than to arouse suspicion by asking what was down there, and waited until the place was quite deserted.

Being the new girl, she found it difficult to break away from the staff restroom, but when she eventually managed to, she was at least sure where they all were. 'There must be an easier way to get down there than through that automatic door,' Gabrielle thought to herself as she wandered round the pink gravelled backyard. Reasoning that there was probably more than one entrance to the basement from outside, she began to pick her way carefully round the house in the slowly descending summer dusk. As though her thoughts had been read, a familiar shape stood waiting for her by an ivy-covered alcove beneath some large French windows. As Toby pointed down into it she at first could see nothing other than the blanket of ivy. But he stood resolutely where he was until she kicked into the growing tangle.

Not only did the ivy buckle, but the surface it was growing over as well. With a hollow cracking sound, an old rotten wooden door fell from its hinges and crashed down a short flight of steps. Gabrielle froze at the noise, sure her discovery of the entrance was not going to be secret much longer. Seeing nowhere to flee but through the ivy curtain and down the steps, she fought her way through the entangled mass, and pulled it back to cover the entrance as best she could when she was through. She waited on the steps, watching through the ivy for a few moments to make sure she had not attracted anyone's attention, then stealthily began to descend into the gloom.

She had forgotten to bring a torch, of course, and was compelled to grope her way along the rough wall at the bottom of the steps until she found herself in an ancient coal cellar. She did not need a degree to know that if she reached up she would find the slanting doors that should have been on the outside of the coal cellar. Not able to immediately fathom out why the coal chute should have been on the inside of the

house, apart from being constructed by a builder with a grudge against the owner, Gabrielle gingerly pushed the doors open. She hauled herself up on to a tiled pathway faintly lit by skylights in the top of a wall. Then she realised that the ground floor of the house had been built over the demolished remains of another building and part of its garden. She even stumbled over ancient flowerpots and garden tools that must have been left there all that time ago.

Not knowing which way to go, it was fortunate that Toby had decided to remain, leading her along the enclosed tiled garden path until they came to a dead end at a rusty grating. It was possible to see through the grating into a dimly lit corridor below, which was long and quite deserted. Not thinking for one moment she could wrench the grating out with her bare hands, Gabrielle half heartedly shook it. To her amazement it came free. It was too much of a coincidence and she turned to look accusingly at Toby, but Toby had gone. His fancy cream shirt and fading frock coat were nowhere to be seen. Things were going too well for Gabrielle's rational mind. The very fact that she was able to get so far so easily made her suspicious when anyone less cautious would have been elated. She pushed her way through the cavity where the grating had been and dropped to the floor below.

Although she was now below ground, the air was quite warm and dry. Gabrielle could hear the faint whirring of an air conditioning fan as she moved carefully up the corridor. The door at the end of it opened without any difficulty, and when she examined the other side of it she could see that the heavy bolt had either been drawn or someone had very conveniently forgotten to secure it. Then she looked ahead to the motionless figure of Toby waiting for her to catch up. He must have been the one making her progress so easy, but she could not fathom how a spirit form could manage acts requiring a good deal of physical strength.

Gabrielle stopped for a moment to think. Could someone be expecting her? How could Humbert know Wendle had

spoken to her unless he had told him? It was not possible, she decided, and followed Toby once more. He soon stopped by a grille at the bottom of the wall and she peered through it into a white-walled room below. Inside were four men. Two were guarding a door, and an obese figure was standing over a form lying on a table. Looking down from where she was Gabrielle could see that the man on the table was Wendle. From the grotesque bloated features of the man by him it was easy to deduce that he was Mr Gunn. He appeared to be frantically trying to wake Wendle up, and as she observed Toby from the corner of her eye she could see him getting fainter and fainter until eventually he vanished and Wendle was brought to his senses by the hefty smack Gunn administered to his face.

'At last,' she could hear Gunn growl. 'Don't think you can get out of this by staying unconscious forever,' he threatened. 'I'm not going to have you killed just yet.'

'Why not?' murmured Wendle, 'Haven't you taken out any insurance on me?'

Gunn clearly did not like this accurate reference to his method of amassing a fortune, and hit out again. By this time Wendle was fully conscious and managed to roll from the table before more damage could be done. He obviously preferred to be asleep, with or without the aid of chloroform.

'I've told you, I don't know anything about this Star Dancer,' Wendle pleaded. 'I wasn't told any more than you, I swear.'

'Of course you were, you lying pup!' Gunn shouted. 'You never did have any respect for me, but I've got too much to lose to put up with your bloodymindedness now.'

'What's the difference if you're going to get a surgeon to remove the transmitter anyway?'

'The difference is whether you get an anaesthetic or not when he does it.'

Gabrielle could see Wendle stiffen at the idea. A nausea in the pit of her stomach told her she would have to do something before the surgeon arrived the next morning.

Gunn continued to rail at his victim like a sadistic spider for as long as his body had the breath, adding a few more threats worse than the one he had already delivered. Then he stormed out, leaving the two guards with Wendle. Gabrielle knew it would have been impossible to get to him from her position. There was nothing but wall, and the grille she was watching through would have needed more than even Toby's supernatural powers to shift it without alerting the guards. There was nothing to do but return to the servants' quarters before she was missed.

8

Gabrielle dared not risk going to sleep for fear of not waking up before morning, or having one of her terrible nightmares. So she sat at the window of her attic bedroom looking up at the shadows of the imitation Tudor beams. She heard the purring of a car engine drawing up in front of the house below her. Carefully edging her window wider, she leaned out to see what could be overheard.

'Couldn't make it sooner,' called a man climbing from the car.

'It's only three,' Gunn's voice came back, but not so loudly. 'Keep it quiet, can't you.' Then, to one of his guards, presumably, he went on, 'Get his equipment.'

'You were joking about the anaesthetic, weren't you?' the visitor inquired apprehensively.

'No. He still hasn't told me anything. Don't start getting squeamish now. You're being paid enough, aren't you?'

'Yes. I'm getting paid enough,' was the resigned reply of a blackmailed man.

Gabrielle did not wait to hear any more. She was stealthily making her way to the hall by the time the surgeon's equipment had been unloaded. She managed to get into the hall and conceal herself beneath the stairs without being seen, but it was impossible for her to enter the automatic doors with the men passing in and out. Then, to her surprise and relief, she glimpsed Wendle's back as he was escorted by two henchmen from the basement and across the hall to another room.

Gabrielle waited till she thought the hall completely empty, then prepared to make her way to the room. Before she could step from the cover of the stairs, though, a familiar

voice behind her said, 'Strange how these warm nights keep one awake, isn't it?'

She spun round in surprise to see Weatherby's mischievous smile beaming at her from the gloom. She should have been terrified, but the fright he gave her made her angry instead. She blurted out, 'What are you doing, sneaking about like that?'

'You're not a laundry maid,' he said. 'You're too grand even to be a lady-in-waiting.'

'And you're not a butler.'

'Then you tell me what I'm doing sneaking about here.'

'How should I know?' she snapped. 'You could be a policeman for all I care.' The smile faded. 'You are a policeman then . . . I thought you were too daft to be a butler.'

'Thanks,' he said, crestfallen. 'And I thought I was going to get a medal out of this.'

'What is your real name then?' Gabrielle demanded.

'Weatherby. What's yours?'

'Jennifer.'

'No, really, it *is* Weatherby.'

'You must be joking.'

He stepped into the hall light and she could see his face. 'You're not kidding are you? Mine's Gabrielle. Why didn't you change your name?'

'It would have meant giving me new cover and that could have been expensive. So, as I didn't come from these parts, it didn't matter too much. It's not as if we thought there was anything too serious going on.'

'Depends on what you call serious.'

'Oh, I can't tell you anything. But you can tell me what you know.'

'I know somebody is going to be murdered in a very short time.' Gabrielle made her way across the hall towards the room where Wendle had been taken.

'Now that could develop into something serious,' Weatherby said, following.

'So what are you going to do about it?'

'I've got to have proof of intent at least,' he hedged. 'How can you be so sure there's going to be a murder?'

'If you know as much as I do,' she decided to gamble, 'then you won't need proof.' Gabrielle clenched her fist and knocked hard on the door, shouting, 'Mr Humbert! I want to talk to you.'

There was a stony silence both inside and outside the room. Weatherby froze momentarily before he dashed to the cover of the stairs again. The door swung open slowly and revealed a circle of amazed expressions. Without being invited, Gabrielle strolled inside and found herself face to face with the grotesque puffy features of Gunn.

'Good morning, Mr Humbert,' she said coolly, realising to her own surprise that she was totally calm, 'I've heard so much about you, I thought it was time we met.'

'Who are you?' blustered Gunn, half outraged and half afraid, 'I don't recollect ever meeting you before?'

'Oh, we've never met. It's just that I've heard so much about you I couldn't resist the temptation of finding out whether it was all true.' Gabrielle had to subdue the urge to look about the room to see where Wendle was. She knew it would have been fatal to show any interest that could have connected them.

'Where did you get that name Humbert from?'

'Oh . . . I'm a journalist. I'm afraid I practised a little deception in applying for a job here as a laundry maid yesterday.' She paused tantalisingly. 'Not so long ago I came across some most fascinating reports about ships lost at sea. And I found some pictures.'

'What ship? What pictures?' snarled Gunn, growing redder and redder.

'Of a Victorian ship and a shipping merchant who looked remarkably like you.'

'Are you trying to blackmail me?' His piggy eyes squinted dangerously.

Gabrielle laughed. 'What, Mr Humbert? In front of all these people?'

'Well, you're not calling on me at this time of night just to get background for a story.'

'You are a difficult man to meet,' she apologised, but sensed the charade was beginning to founder like one of his insured ships.

'Him!' Gunn suddenly roared, pointing to Wendle. 'You're here because of him!'

'Who?' inquired Gabrielle innocently, and let her gaze follow his pointing finger.

When she saw Wendle's face, though, her coolness was transformed to blazing fury. He had been bruised and cut nearly beyond recognition. She should have been terrified, but all she could feel was uncontrolled rage rising from the pit of her stomach.

'Get her out of here,' Gunn roared to one of his guards, who looked like a cross between the side of a house and a sewer rat. But before he could lay a finger on her he was stopped in his ungainly tracks by a sight more alarming than an angry Gabrielle. A sudden explosion of fire engulfed one of the heavy velvet curtains and reduced it to ashes in a matter of seconds.

'What the hell was that?' yelled one of the guards in alarm.

'The place is on fire!' called back another with a little more perception, 'Get the hose.'

'Fire be damned,' shouted the surgeon. 'That was an explosion. I'm getting out of here, Gunn.' He snatched up a bag of his most valuable tools and made for the door.

'If anyone tries to leave I'll kill them,' threatened Gunn, taking a pistol from his inside pocket.

Gabrielle was wondering how Weatherby had achieved the explosion without even being in the room but, as Gunn poured out a stream of hysterical words, she began to understand.

'It's here!' he screamed. 'The transmitter brought it here. Can't you see? Put him in the middle of the room away from

everyone else, you idiots, before it incinerates all of us as well!'

Without knowing what Gunn was ranting about, one of the guards seized hold of Wendle and hurled him to the floor in the centre of the room. As the men moved away from him Gabrielle suspected she would be safer with Wendle. She dashed to him before anyone could stop her.

'Get her out of here, can't you!' Gunn screamed again, and the same henchman who had tried to eject her previously moved forward.

Just then a column of white fire soared from the floor of the room and burned away the ground he was about to tread on. It seared his eyebrows and he ran from the room shrieking in terror.

As all this was happening Weatherby bounced in and enquired innocently, 'What's the matter, Mr Gunn? I thought I smelled burning.'

'Mind your own business, you interfering imbecile!' snapped Gunn. 'Phone Mrs Tavistock and tell her . . .'

'I really think we should phone the fire brigade instead, Mr Gunn,' waffled Weatherby.

'Don't argue!' Gunn cuffed him so hard round the ear he almost fell over.

Meanwhile, the other guards and the surgeon managed to escape from the gradually spreading flames. When Gunn raised his pistol again, he discovered his captive audience had gone. Even his limited comprehension told him that the room was on fire, and if he wanted to save the transmitter attracting the Star Dancer, he would have to save Wendle as well.

'Pick him up,' Gunn ordered Weatherby, waving the pistol at him. 'Bring him outside.'

Weatherby did not need telling twice. Carefully he made his way past the flames to Gabrielle and took off his jacket to wrap round Wendle's shoulders.

'It's all right,' he hissed to Gabrielle. 'There's no need to

worry about a thing,' and smiled in a way that confirmed her doubts about his sanity.

'Outside! Outside!' snapped Gunn as Weatherby picked up Wendle with surprising ease. 'Keep him away from me though.' He backed into the hall, where the rest of the staff were too busy evacuating the building to pay any attention to what he was doing.

Although Weatherby had seemed to lift Wendle with ease, Gabrielle saw him falter at the door of the room, perhaps unsure which way to turn. As he did so, another column of fire leapt up before the front door and blocked their way. Gunn was nearest at the time and began to panic, screaming, 'Get rid of him! Get rid of him! Keep him away from me!'

'Why don't you make up your mind?' Weatherby shouted back in exasperation.

'Looks as though we're all trapped now,' Gabrielle told him as smokeless flames licked round the entrance to the staff quarters. 'Fires must have started simultaneously in a dozen different places.'

'How often do buildings burn down after you've been employed in them for a day?' asked Weatherby, but before she could answer, Gunn was taking aim at Wendle and squeezing the trigger.

'Look out!' she called, dragging them both to the floor.

Gunn, from the middle of the hall, took aim again—then his body shuddered violently in a spasm, as though his whole bloated being was contracting.

'What's happening?' gasped Gabrielle, but Weatherby was speechless as he watched Gunn's body shrivel until his outsize clothes hung on him like a collapsed tent. His features shrank too until there was no flesh between his skin and the skull beneath it. The creature that was Gunn stood against the background of the burning hall for a few seconds, then collapsed to dust, which swirled about in the heat of the flames.

Gabrielle and Weatherby were aware that their situation was potentially no better. The intense smokeless flames that

had been licking around the hall, were now roaring. The upper floors were alight and about to collapse as well. They couldn't see any available window to climb out of, and even the basement was belching fire. They were beginning to have every reason to think they were not going to survive the rest of the night, when a loud noise thundered past them.

It seemed they were actually able to see the sound as it struck against the smouldering wallpaper and plaster by the front entrance. The wall had been delivered a tremendous blow and a hole sheared right through the masonry to safety outside.

Not waiting to see how the miracle had been achieved, Weatherby and Gabrielle staggered through the hole, carrying Wendle. They sat huddled with the rest of the staff a safe distance away while the local fire crew tried to pump water on the blaze by putting a filter in the nearest lily pond. Without a mains hydrant, however, there was not enough pressure for the water from the hoses to reach the first storey. By the time other pumps arrived the building was a pile of smouldering rubble, punctuated by the skeletal remains of chimney stacks.

'Never known a fire burn like that before,' Gabrielle overheard a fire officer remark to a policeman. 'Even the masonry couldn't take the heat. Seems like a fishy one to me.'

At that moment Gabrielle was just relieved to be alive, and did not even have the energy to argue with Weatherby.

Somehow, in the anticlimax that followed, she remembered Penny's bike. She expected to find it incinerated along with everything else that had been near the house, but to her relief it had been shielded from the blaze by the stone walls of the shed it had been stowed in. She allowed an obliging policeman to cram it, partially successfully, into the boot of a police car while she flopped on to the back seat and dozed most of the way back to the cottage. Weatherby had taken Wendle for hospital treatment, promising to phone to let her know how he was.

About nine o'clock the following morning the phone in the hall rang, and Gabrielle, who had somehow stayed awake to wait for it, lifted the receiver and managed to murmur the number. Weatherby sounded as sickeningly cheerful as ever and told her that Wendle was in much better condition than could have been expected, and was due to be discharged later that day. If she had not been so tired, Gabrielle would have been surprised. She muttered her approval when he asked if he could bring him to the cottage so she could keep an eye on him as he had no next of kin, nor friends. Apparently Weatherby, still had more investigating to do on the case, and would not be free for a couple of days.

It was not until after a refreshing few hours snooze that Gabrielle thought there was anything odd about about the conversation with Weatherby. After Gunn's death, what else could be so important that he had to dash off and investigate it — and why should Wendle not be just as safe either in hospital or his own bungalow? It was evident when Wendle did arrive in a police car that he did not think much of the idea either. His wits had returned with a vengeance after the night's experience, and he seemed more furious than thankful at the risk Gabrielle had taken to save him. The unsightly bruises he had sustained were just patches of discoloration on his face and his cool manner had not been warmed up by his near roasting. Gabrielle suspected that he was still worried about something, so she asked, 'How much does Weatherby know about you and what started the fire?'

'He was investigating insurance frauds. For all he knows he still is,' was the stiff reply. 'I haven't told him anything to make him think differently.'

'Perhaps just as well.'

'He'll be coming back here to talk to you when he has the time of course,' Wendle reminded her, then suddenly added, 'Get well away from this place before he does.'

Gabrielle did not believe her ears. 'Don't be so ruddy daft! What on earth are you talking about?'

'While you're near me you're in danger. I told you I didn't

want you to take any risks.'

'Given the way things happened, I didn't have much choice!'

'You don't know what you're doing, taking chances like that. You're a silly little fool. You should get as far away from here as you can before your luck runs out as well.'

'Don't preach at me!' Gabrielle stormed back at him, the lack of proper sleep putting her in an unreasonable mood. 'You're the one who got me involved in this, remember.'

'I made a mistake. I should have told you nothing.'

'Well it's a bit late to realise that now,' she declared with finality, and marched into the kitchen to wash up the plates left over from the last two days.

'Things are going to get worse,' he called after her. 'There's nothing I can do about this Star Dancer. You saw what it was capable of last night.' There was no reply apart from the clattering of crockery in the kitchen and the screaming of seagulls outside.

9

The six-hoofed Kyrupa galloped round and round the shattered refractor station as though they knew it was only a matter of time before they became the most intelligent species on Ojal. In the midst of their fertile grazing land of shimmering herbs, the remains of the station's domed refractor shields lay twisted and seared. Chief Controller Opu had been catapulted halfway across the planet on a travel beam to survey the damage and try to restore the gradually diminishing confidence of the station crews dotted about the globe. It had not been her first priority, but a sinister lull in the attacks of the Star Dancer had given her the opportunity. She doubted that the intermission in its activity was due to any success the Kybion had been having on Perimeter 84926. Taigal Rax had still heard nothing from it, and the machine's competence was in doubt. It must have been malfunctioning and, that being the case, she and many others would probably never live to know the reason why.

In an attempt to prevent the Star Dancer sucking their energy pool dry, this particular station had tried to close its refractor shields, and the disagreement they had had with the marauding creature had left them scattered in many pieces about the otherwise peaceful countryside.

'Well, it was worth a try, I suppose,' Opu told the staff, wondering how anyone could have been so stupid. 'Looks as though you're out of commission from now on. Stand by, though, we may get the better of the creature yet. It seems to be either giving up or occupied elsewhere at the moment,' she reassured them, wishing somebody would do the same for her.

Opu finished surveying the damage and remaining operational stations, and returned to her own base, winging her

way over the Ojalies preparing to sunbathe. She wanted to do a personal check of the shields before the next onslaught.

'Couldn't be caused by a freak storm of collapsars about the size of atoms, do you think?' said a familiar voice from the other side of one of the perilously high shields.

Opu looked up to see the furiously fluttering wings of Annac as she clung to the slippery surface.

'We would have picked up anything like that before it reached the edge of the solar system,' she sighed. 'What are you doing up here? It's dangerous, even without an alien monster zooming in and out.'

'I know how everything works,' Annac assured her haughtily. 'I've got to be somewhere.'

'Why not visit Anaru?'

'I think she's having some success,' Annac told her almost disapprovingly. 'She keeps telling me to go away. My brain may be old, but it knows things you two'll never guess.'

'Does it know how to pull you out of a straight plunge to the ground when your wings decide they've had enough?'

'I've been over and inside this thing thousands of times,' Annac protested.

'It must have had a lot wrong with it then.'

'From where I am now,' Annac observed thoughtfully, 'I would say you are losing your sense of humour.'

'I am also losing my sanity!' Opu responded so loudly some of the gathering sunbathers half a mile below them must have heard. 'Let's get out of here before the sun comes up.'

As she guided the unsteady Annac to the ground, Opu asked, 'How do you mean, Anaru's having some success?'

'How should I know?' protested Annac. 'She won't let me in to find out.'

'She hasn't managed to contact anything in the vicinity of the Kybion has she?'

'I suppose that's what it's all about. That was what she was trying to do.' She looked at Opu. 'Why? Why shouldn't she be able to pick anything on its co-ordinates?' Opu was suspiciously silent, and Annac suddenly understood. 'You

haven't heard anything from it yourself, have you?' she asked.

'Taigal Rax still haven't been able to contact the android,' Opu admitted quietly as they touched ground. 'Don't raise your voice and let everyone else know.' She hustled her inside the station.

'The thing could be malfunctioning,' Opu whispered, her voice echoing in the cool lobby below the control room. 'Or it just hasn't been able to trace the Star Dancer, or it has and hasn't been able to do anything about it.'

'Why couldn't it do anything about it? Its power units could blot out a white dwarf at close range. It should easily have neutralised the thing by now.'

'Assuming the Star Dancer consisted of something we are familiar with. We may think we're pretty clever, but we've never travelled from our planet. The only knowledge we have of the rest of the galaxy comes to us in pictures and impulses. Our senses have never experienced different life forms, other than those who have been capable of reaching us.'

'Never thought of it quite like that, I suppose what you take for granted does somehow seem permanent. Taigal Rax knows this world though. They should have a better idea than we do. Why haven't they come up with any suggestions?'

'They're still trying to fathom out why the Kybion hasn't contacted them,' Opu told Annac. 'If they want more information that some simple submerged service robot can supply they will have to use the Kybini System to transmit the equipment, and that would break the legal level of time interference. I only know that whatever happens to us, Taigal Rax will have to send out the robots they have on Perimeter 84926 to dismantle the wretched android if they don't hear from it soon. For all we know it could be behaving in a way that would attract the attention of a Watcher.'

'Then they'll probably end up in the same neutron stew as us,' commented Annac as they walked up the ramp to the higher levels.

As the benign but unnourishing pink sun set, Opu watched the vibrant rays of its yellow energy-giving companion probe their way above the horizon for another turbulent shift. As time trickled past, things were so nerve-shatteringly quiet Opu kept sending out directives to the other stations to keep them occupied and alert. She sensed danger in the air.

When the thunderbolt struck she was almost relieved. The creature had come in many guises, but this was the most violent yet. It crashed through the refractor and energy pool of a major station like a battering ram. The staff had fled to the shelter beneath it, and came out shocked to find the glistening refractor shields shattered. Opu's sharp reflexes had held in the fail safe device for as long as she dared, while the demolished station was isolated from the grid, but she knew this to be the last straw. From now on the loss of power could not be replaced and the whole system would slowly wind down.

Annac heard Opu observe in a low voice, 'Looks as though it's turned really nasty on us this time. It's never behaved like that before, even when it broke through the shields of Station 73.'

'Wonder what could have upset it?' Annac pondered aloud.

'If we don't find out soon, we'll all be knowing what our ancestors felt like when there was a slow eclipse.'

'That could be unpleasant . . .' mused Annac. 'It's been estimated their survival chances were only fifty percent. Lucky they didn't have them very often.'

The rest of the shift passed without incident, but the irreparable damage had been done. With seven stations completely gone, and the rest with only half-full energy pools, it was computed that the species had only a matter of suns before the reserves were hopelessly depleted. Even if the Star Dancer's attacks stopped, the lost power could not be replaced in time.

If things had not been so desperate, Opu might have ignored the message from Anaru, which simply said 'contact

made'. Although there was only a very remote chance the seer and her primitive equipment could help the situation, Opu stealthily left the control after the yellow shift, careful not to let Annac know where she had gone.

The large circular room was now cluttered with even more apparatus, and Opu could see Anaru sitting motionless on the floor through the light beam curtain. Several different light sources were playing about her head. As Anaru looked round and saw Opu, she slapped the flat control disc and shut them down. 'Come in,' she said with a marked lack of the ebullience that was part of her nature. 'I'm not sure whether you are going to like this or not.'

Her manner was quite off-putting; Opu had been hoping for a more enthusiastic reception, possibly heralding good news.

'What's wrong?' she asked.

'I've managed to contact a human on Perimeter 84926.'

'And?'

'And I'm not too sure about it at all.'

'Why not?' Opu sat down next to her.

'I can't tell myself,' she explained. 'I've never seen a creature like it before, but Healphani joined the loop to observe what was going on. She says it's female'.

'And?'

'She reckons we've got a bad one.'

'Why?' demanded Opu.

'There's something about the creature that doesn't seem right. Although Healphani can't tell exactly, it seems this human understood what we were telling it a bit too quickly. It looks somehow wrong to her.'

'You managed to pick it up by following the Kybion's trace?'

'Oh yes. If she's somehow contacted the Kybion it might account for her familiarity with the situation. The human's also managed to rig up some primitive apparatus to boost her own transmitting power.'

'I don't like the sound of that either. This might have

something to do with why the Kybion hasn't been able to contact Taigal Rax . . . If it is, we are on very sticky ground. If these humans are as potentially untrustworthy as we've been told, it could be more than dangerous if they have managed to interfere with the android.'

'That's not possible, surely?' asked Anaru in disbelief.

'I wouldn't have thought so before now.' She grimaced. 'But I'm beginning to have doubts about a lot of things at the moment. Can I talk to this human?'

'Yes.'

Anaru dashed off to her alcove for a few seconds to raise Healphani and ask her to listen in without the human knowing. She then returned to switch on the multi beam power fields which played about their heads.

'Think simple thoughts,' Anaru warned Opu. 'They only have a brain capacity a fraction of ours.'

'Just more cunning perhaps,' Opu said to herself as an indistinct human image flickered on to the screen.

'Thank you for waiting,' she could hear Anaru's thoughts say, 'I have the someone of importance you wanted to speak to here.'

Trapped on the thought loop as she was, Opu was not able to comment on Anaru's little deception, but was compelled to think a simple question at the screen.

'What is your name, human?' before the shape had become very clear.

'Tas . . . Tas . . .' She heard the apparatus splutter, then recover. 'Tasmin is my spirit name.'

'Why do you want to contact me, Tasmin?'

'It is you who want to contact me.'

Opu would make no further comment until she knew what this self-assured human looked like. With the image sharper, Opu was able to see the remarkably small skull of a creature wearing something very elaborate piled on top of its head. It had no wings. The face had white eyes with coloured dots in the middle of them, a feature jutting from the centre, and a wide red split beneath. And it was a very odd colour, though

that could have been due to the distance and the apparatus the image was coming through.

'Why do I want to speak to you, Tasmin?' Opu asked at length. 'I doubt if you even know my name.'

'Your name does not matter. If you are the most important person on your planet at the moment you will want to speak to me. I know what you are looking for and where it can be found.'

'Then you know where the Kybion is?'

'The Kybion?' The red gash beneath the human's nose moved upwards at the corners. 'I do not know or care where that deficient machine is.'

Opu's brain worked feverishly as she tried to shield her thoughts. Tasmin clearly knew about the Kybion, and was telling her she considered it to be harmless; she must know something of even greater importance. She thought so quickly that Tasmin was not able to understand, and the screen flickered furiously.

'Don't do that,' Anaru warned. 'Concentrate.'

Opu pulled her bubbling thoughts together, and demanded, 'What is it we are looking for, then?'

'A source of such immense energy that it can travel the galaxy and destroy the life on your planet if it wanted,' the image replied.

'You make it sound as though it had a will of its own?'

'If I knew where it is, we might be able to control it.'

'That I find difficult to believe.'

'Your machine, the Kybion, over a century ago fitted a young man with the transmitter you designed to attract it,' Tasmin explained. 'It gave him and three more people longevity. One of those people recently kidnapped the young man, but before he could cut the transmitter from his body, the Star Dancer you are looking for arrived and sent his house up in flames. It didn't do Mr Humbert much good at all I understand, but he was such an impulsive, greedy person he probably deserved it. Now the other two of us have a much better idea.'

'Oh yes?' Opu did not need Healphani to tell her what was coming next.

'If you were to give us the knowledge and power to control it on this planet, you wouldn't have to worry any more.'

Opu replied, 'We'll think about it,' and broke out of the loop, letting Anaru complete the conversation.

'Now don't go too far away will you, Tasmin?' She saw Opu waving her hand, telling her to get rid of the human. Tasmin faded from the screen, and Anaru closed down her power beam to speak to Healphani. At that, Opu rejoined the loop.

'Well?' Opu asked, even before Healphani was able to come into focus. 'What did you make of that?'

'We believe that this human female is indulging in a practice widely used on her planet,' Healphani said. 'It is called blackmail.'

'Go on.'

'We suspect that were you to supply her with the knowledge and power she required, she would not use it for the purpose she indicated.'

'Strangely enough I got the same impression. Assuming we had that knowledge and power, we would have to transmit it through you. I hope you would not agree to help us?'

'You can be sure of that.'

'Thanks.' Opu again left the loop, letting Anaru shut the equipment down.

Opu sat silently thinking over what she had discovered during the conversation. Although there was nothing hopeful in it, she at least understood a little more of what had been happening. The Kybion had involved four humans for some reason. One carrying the transmitter, one apparently dead, and the remaining two trying to blackmail enough power from her to hold their own world to ransom. Where was the android though? And why didn't Tasmin seem to know exactly what the Star Dancer was? It must have had some sort of form that could have been recognised. Or perhaps it

69

was something alien to Perimeter 84926 and had decided to make its home there?

'If you don't learn to stop thinking so quickly you could damage the equipment,' Opu became aware of Anaru scolding.

'It's a pity I can't damage the brain on the other end of it,' Opu wished out loud.

'Well, you can't. There are safety gates in the power field to protect smaller intellects.' Anaru added as an afterthought, 'And they cannot be removed.'

'Well, at least we know what probably happened to the Kybion,' Opu admitted grudgingly.

'Don't be too despondent,' Anaru replied, seeming to return to her natural self. 'If we have managed to get through to this human, there might be a chance of contacting another.'

'What other? Another one as devious as that? Or one that doesn't know anything about what we are trying to find out?'

'I have a feeling . . .' Anaru's orange eyes lit like flares, 'I have a feeling we are closer than we think.'

'Is it possible to get any closer?'

'If we let this human think she has convinced us. We may be able to insist on contacting the human who has the transmitter.'

Opu hesitated for a second, beginning to see the value in the idea.

'If we were able to isolate the human with the transmitter,' Opu pondered, 'then we would also be able to isolate the energy source. And if the Star Dancer did have some sort of intelligence . . . we might be able to make a mind link with it. The only problem is . . .'

'What?'

'Who is going to be the one to contact it and have their brains blasted through the back of their skull?'

Anaru obviously had not thought of that. Her impression of the universe was a benign one.

'Still,' continued Opu, 'It seems like the only chance we have.'

'What do you want me to do?' asked Anaru apprehensively.

'I'll give you the simple co-ordinates of the transmitter's signal. It won't interfere with its function if you give them to Tasmin and let her transmit them. This should bring the human with the transmitter to her and give her some proof of our trust. Make it clear that if she harms the male human, the transmitter will cease to function. She will probably be scared enough to believe it after what happened to their other associate.'

'It is very deceitful.'

'What else can we do? We are obviously not dealing with straightforward beings.' Then, as an afterthought, she added 'Don't tell Annac what we're up to, will you?'

'Not if you don't want,' Anaru agreed. 'I'll let you know through your control console as soon as anything happens.'

10

Day and night passed in the cottage and Gabrielle and Wendle had hardly exchanged a word since their argument. Wendle spent most of the time dozing or writing letters and Gabrielle read. The only thing to break the monotony for her was the fancy that she could remember a little of one of her dreams. She had been listening to a soft mocking voice, but was unable to remember who owned it. It seemed to be explaining some symbols to her: 'This was the shape which makes atoms fly apart, this the one which can stop time. Another to slow down a rotating pulsar . . .' Astronomy was not her subject however. She returned to her book and easily forgot the ghostly lesson.

Eventually the strain of the silence between them, punctuated only by the seagulls and an insistently chirping sparrow, broke Gabrielle's resolve to remain quiet. Pushing a cup of tea under the dozing Wendle's nose, she announced, 'I'm fed up. I feel like going for a walk. Want to come?'

Wendle looked up at her through half-closed eyes as though examining her motives. Deciding they were genuine, he inclined his head in agreement.

'I know a quiet walk across country in the direction of the town, where we won't bump into anyone,' he suggested.

'Far?'

'Far enough,' he answered non-committally, his bruised face still making it difficult for him to talk.

'We'd better leave a message for Weatherby to let him know where we are, in case he decides to turn up.'

'Hang Weatherby.'

Gabrielle thought that this solution sounded a bit drastic. While Wendle was posting the letters he'd written the previous night, at the railway post box, she wrote a short note

saying they had gone for a walk in the direction Wendle had indicated, which she tucked under the weighty door knocker. After walking side by side in silence for some while, Gabrielle thought it safe to ask, 'Feeling better?'

'Yes,' murmured Wendle, hardly opening his mouth. 'You?'

'Yes,' Gabrielle knew he was asking if she was still angry with him. 'Do you still want me to get as far away from here as possible?'

'It's probably too late now anyway,' Wendle gave a short sigh.

'But this Star Dancer hasn't bothered us since the other night. It might have been the fact you were in danger that sparked it off.'

'Probably.'

'So if it looks after you like that, why should I worry about it?'

For the first time since she'd known him Wendle smiled. It may have been a tight wry smile, but it transformed his face. There was an aura about him which she found both intriguing and chilling, as though his presence should have made her aware of some cosmic crime. The sensation fled when Wendle spoke.

'I didn't want to see you come to any harm. You've got a long while to live yet. And I've lived too long. It would be stupid if you were to get killed protecting me.'

'Never thought of it like that. Seems unfair that you were never able to make use of your longevity like the other three, though. Not that I think you'd be dishonest, but you should have been allowed a little fun. Were you married when it happened?'

'No, I was never married. I fell in love though. After all this time I can still remember that.'

'What happened?'

'Nothing.'

'Nothing?'

'Nemesis sent me a Valentine instead.'

'Wasn't there anyone else?'

'Yes. Some while before then.'

'Didn't she love you enough?' asked Gabrielle.

'Over a century ago, girls married who their fathers allowed them to,' Wendle explained flatly.

'Oh yes . . . I've heard of something like that nearer home.' Wendle looked at her quizzically. 'Perhaps I was lucky, but I shouldn't think of it like that.'

'You'd never make a good wife. You've too much mind of your own.'

'I can't have children anyway.'

'Oh?'

'I was in a car crash when I was four. There was one other side effect too.'

'What was that?'

'Nightmares,' Gabrielle told him. 'Ever since I can remember I have been having nightmares.'

'What about?'

'I can never remember. I only know I've just had one when I wake up either sweating or screaming. Even had to have a room to myself in the children's home because of it. That was good, I suppose.'

'Nightmares are terrible things to have. I used to have them until I managed to consciously leave my body.'

'Good trick that,' grinned Gabrielle at the thought of Toby. 'You should teach me.'

'You prefer him to me, don't you?' Wendle suddenly asked.

Gabrielle was stunned by the question for a moment. 'But you are Toby.'

'Not any more, sometimes I think he died of fright that night of the shipwreck.'

'Where is the entrance to the tunnel through the cliff?' Gabrielle asked, to break the uneasy silence.

'Near here. That's how I know this walk.'

'Let's go there.'

Wendle, not keen on the idea, stopped for a moment. 'No,

no, I've not been down there since that night.'

'Why not?' asked Gabrielle in amazement.

Wendle did not reply, but remained stock still. Some of the colour left the bruises on his face.

'Surely that's the best way to find the Kybion? I thought that was the most important thing now.'

Wendle still hesitated. 'Have you ever been scared . . . terrified out of your wits?' he asked.

'Well . . . no,' confessed Gabrielle.

'Fear can make people irrational. Unlike pain, which is difficult to remember because it only makes an impression on the body, fear stamps its imprint on the mind. If I survived to be a thousand years old, the fear of that night would still be there.' Wendle smiled briefly. 'No — you don't understand, do you? You'll never be afraid of anything.'

'Should I be?'

'No. Stay the way you are. Fear is a useless commodity.'

'Show me where the tunnel is.'

Wendle walked ahead and led her through a meadow and on to a narrow overgrown path. They went some way along an old disused railway track and through a dangerously crumbling tunnel to emerge in a bewildering undergrowth of brambles and shrubs growing on the embankment. Wendle pointed halfway up the slope. Gabrielle clawed her way through the vegetation to find a slab of rock which had already been cleared of obstructing weeds.

'Someone's been here quite recently,' she called back to Wendle.

'Are you sure?' he asked, catching her up.

'There's nothing growing over this rock that hasn't been pulled over it deliberately.' She seized a corner to try and budge it and pushed it far enough aside to make a crack for her to squeeze through. Before she entered, Gabrielle peered inside. She saw a long dimly lit corridor straight ahead.

'Don't go down there please,' Wendle implored her. 'It can't be safe.'

'If it isn't, I'll come out again,' she assured him. 'It's all right. It's lit and looks quite safe,' she went on as she eased herself inside. 'I won't be long.'

Wendle stood watching impassively through the gap as she jogged down the long corridor into the heart of the cliffs.

Of course, Gabrielle had not taken into consideration what she would say to the Kybion if she did meet it, except 'Hello, the Star Dancer's found your transmitter and you'd better go and take it off Wendle quick.' She was too fascinated by her surroundings to be bothered with such academic matters. The corridor was very long, but fortunately the floor was even, and sloped downwards at a slight angle. Eventually she came to several small caverns. They would have been ideal for smugglers, but she did not see any contraband in them; they appeared to be quite empty. She walked through into a larger chamber where there seemed to be fittings of some sort. She was unable to make out what they were, and pressed and pulled a few small prominences in the wall to see what would happen. Each time she did so, a cavity behind the rock face was illuminated to show more objects she was unable to identify. Tiring of the game, she moved into the next chamber and discovered the place where she imagined Toby and his companions must have met the Kybion.

A wide platform ran along the back of the chamber. Part of it was filled with water, and led presumably to the exit to the sea on the opposite side. Gabrielle walked along the platform examining more of the wall cavities. When she had reached the far end she heard a movement behind her. Not knowing if she was up to meeting a faceless android, she turned very, very slowly to see what was cutting off her escape from the chamber. In the dim light she could see a tall dark motionless figure by the entrance. She called out in creaking tones, 'Who is it?'

'Only me,' sang out a familiar voice. 'I saw your note and followed you.'

'Weatherby! You scared me half to death! Why follow me all the way down here anyway?'

'Well, Mr Wendle thought you'd been gone a long while, and I could tell he didn't want to come down himself, so . . .' His words trailed off and he shrugged. 'Strange sort of place this. How did you find it?'

'We were just walking. Couldn't you have waited till we got back?'

'Well, I've got this inquisitive nature you see, and . . . '

'And you thought that as you didn't trust either of us, you would just follow and see where we went?'

'Something like that,' Weatherby admitted as she sailed past him back to the other caverns. 'You've got to admit that you and your frosty friend are a pretty suspicious pair. How am I supposed to know what you were up to the other night?'

'You're a detective aren't you?' Her determined stride made him break into a trot to keep up with her.

'You're still sore at me for making you jump the other night.'

'No, it's the fact you seem to make a habit of it.'

'What is this place anyway?' he asked in an offhand way, but she was not fooled that easily.

'I thought you would be able to tell me. Is Wendle still waiting out there?'

'I should think so. I hope he is. It looks as though he could still be in trouble if what I've found out is true.'

'What have you found out?' Before he could tell her it was confidential Gabrielle added, 'Remember what I did last time you wouldn't share a secret with me?'

'I can't tell you. Under that gleaming armour you're probably a nice sort of girl, and I wouldn't want to see anything happen to you.'

'Why should it?' she demanded.

'Because you don't have any sense of danger. You behave as though you could walk on water if the fancy took you,' he told her.

'You nearly scared me to death on two occasions,' she accused him.

'That's different. I've got certificates from arch villains to

prove I'm harmless. But it's unnatural for anyone not to have a sense of danger, like you.'

'Perhaps I'm just as impervious as my gleaming armour.'

On the long way back, Gabrielle found herself breaking into a run. For some inexplicable reason she knew she must hurry. At last she was squeezing back through the entrance and leaping down the embankment. There was no sign of Wendle anywhere. She stood still, looking about, until Weatherby called for her to come and help him through the narrow gap.

'How on earth did you manage to get in there?' she asked absently as she helped pull him through. When he was safely out, she continued, 'Sure you don't want to share your secret now?'

'Eh?' said Weatherby.

'He's gone.'

'Oh hell . . .'

'It hardly surprises me. He was telling me to get as far away from here as possible only yesterday.'

'That so . . .?' Weatherby mused interestedly, 'I wonder why he would tell you that? I can't see any reason unless he was secretly fond of you and getting over-protective.'

'That I doubt,' Gabrielle laughed. 'If so, he certainly kept it secret.' Weatherby seemed reluctant to move while she was still there. 'It's all right, I won't try following you.' She turned and strode off through the old railway tunnel and out of sight.

11

Wendle could dimly remember collapsing on someone's doorstep after his ten-mile forced walk. He had not wanted to take a step of it himself, but something far stronger than his willpower had dragged him ruthlessly through rough countryside and narrow lanes until he looked like a tramp who had been on a route march. His usual immaculate appearance was dishevelled, and his hair tangled and matted with perspiration. Now his head throbbed as though something had been trying to draw his brain out with a magnet. He came to fully, smelling the heavy perfume of incense, and glimpsed a green velvet tablecloth, and a panelled and tassel-strewn room. Everything about it was so overpowering he had no difficulty in passing out again.

The next thing he knew was a voice, which seemed to be a great distance away, saying, 'Hello Toby . . .'

The woman speaking to him was standing in front of a window in the direct sunlight so he could only see her shape at first. Then she moved towards him.

'Did you sleep well?' she asked smoothly, her crinkled hand carefully pushing the hair from his face. Wendle looked up at the woman, who resembled an elderly carrot.

'Mrs Angel!' he suddenly blurted out.

'Used to be, Toby. Mrs Tavistock now.' She traced a magenta-nailed finger round his face. 'After all these years you've still kept your looks, haven't you? Even poor Tasmin hasn't had that much luck.'

'Why can't I move?' Wendle demanded as he realised his limbs would not obey him.

'Don't worry about that, Toby. No one is going to hurt you. Not like that horrible Mr Humbert. He told us all about

what he intended to do to you. Going up in smoke served him right.'

'How did you know? You must have been playing at mediums to have found that out.'

'Oh no,' she laughed ominously. 'That nice Mr Weatherby paid us a visit the other day. Spent quite a time with us, he did.'

'Aren't you worried he might be back then?'

'Goodness no. He'll certainly be back, but he won't bother us. He's only interested in insurance frauds and sunken ships. Don't worry so much, everything is going to be all right.' Mrs Tavistock's discoloured face wrinkled into a frighteningly insincere smile which told Wendle he was not going to have much luck at her hands either.

'What are you going to do with me?' he demanded.

'Nothing. We have been told we must take special care of you. And as long as you help us, that's just what we'll do.'

Wendle did not bother to answer. He closed his eyes and turned away from her. Eventually he heard the rustling of her antique taffeta gown as she moved away and he sighed in relief. From then on Wendle was determined to stay awake for fear of Toby getting the better of his conscious judgement and warning Gabrielle where he was. If he was going to be rescued this time, it would have to be by Weatherby.

By the next morning Gabrielle realised Toby was not going to contact her. She was angry, but knew it was not surprising after the way Wendle had warned her to keep out of trouble. She had dreamed once again though, and this time she could remember most of it. It seemed to her that some new apparition was trying to attract her attention now Toby would no longer respond. She could even recall its name . . . Vian Solran, and vaguely imagined Wendle had been the first one to mention it to her. The creature told Gabrielle that it used to eat stars, but she laughed, and the ghostly visitor laughed with her. A deity that had the power to destroy suns

had swapped that ability for a sense of humour. This was the creature that had shown her those symbols. Again she found herself immersed in the same lesson: 'This is the one that can blow comet tails into life, this the one to gather up untidy asteroids, and this to . . .' While she listened, Gabrielle plucked a symbol from the cloud of codes swimming before her. 'No, no,' said the deity. 'This one is for you.' The one Gabrielle held suddenly changed into something far less spectacular. 'Keep it until you need it.'

'Need it?'

'Oh yes. You will need it . . .'

Clutching her dream symbol Gabrielle slowly woke to discover she was holding a notepad. Disappointed that Toby had not given her any message to write on it, she could do nothing but idle the hours away in the hope Weatherby might contact her. About midday she was even more restless, and so annoyed that she resolved to get on the first train and visit any place on the map that took her fancy. Perhaps it was right to let them both get on with things in the way they thought best.

Gabrielle tidied herself up, locked the cottage and made her way to the station reading Penny's map. She saw that one of the villages on the local line lay next to a lake. This seemed like a cool quiet spot to spend the rest of the day, so she bought a return ticket and sat basking in the sun waiting for the slow train to arrive.

Wendle resisted the urge to try and put up a fight when a man and a woman dressed as nurses came to give him another of the injections that kept his mind awake and his body asleep. He thought it would be wiser to save his energy for when Weatherby turned up . . . if Weatherby turned up.

After a few minutes, to his surprise, he found he was able to stand and walk from the room with the aid of the two attendants. He was led along a wide corridor lined with gilt framed mirrors and down several steps into a lower room.

The air inside smelt of freesias and he felt strangely at ease and comfortable as he was carefully placed in a leather armchair facing a transparent box full of copper coils. The table that supported the equipment was circular. Mrs Tavistock sat one side of it, and facing her across it was . . .

'Tasmin!' 'Wendle blurted out drunkenly. 'How . . .?'

'A girl has to make a living, my precious,' she smiled.

'But — like this?'

Wendle wished sufficient eloquence would return to him so he would not appear such a fool. He could read the comtempt on Tasmin's heavily painted face.

'You're still a dreamer aren't you?' She laughed.

'You've changed . . .'

'As you're in no condition to say anything intelligent, Toby,' warned Mrs Tavistock, 'be quiet.'

'What's this?' Wendle asked as one of the nurses placed apparatus which felt like earphones over his head.

'It's just something we want you to talk to someone through, Toby,' Wendle could hear Tasmin's voice explain over the head gear. 'Don't be alarmed by it. We promise it won't hurt you at all. We have discovered some friends many millions of miles away from here.' She spoke as though she were talking to a six-year-old rather than a man who had lived for a hundred and twenty-seven years. 'We can't see them, I'm afraid, but they have proved that we can trust them. They want to help you out of the dreadful difficulty that terrible machine put you in.'

'This equipment will help you concentrate,' Mrs Tavistock explained. 'You will hear someone ask you questions as though they were talking inside your head. You only need think your replies. Don't try to fight the machine. It is very powerful and could fry your brain if you do not do exactly as you are told. Do you understand?'

'Why?' murmured Wendle.

'I'm not explaining it all again,' snapped Tasmin.

'Why what, Toby?' asked Mrs Tavistock.

'Changed . . . she's changed.'

'Don't be foolish. No one has remained in love with the same person for over a century.' She waved to a nurse. 'He's becoming distraught. Give him another injection.'

Cold numbing desolation returned and Wendle's ability to make sense of his own words fled.

He watched, speechless, as Tasmin pressed a switch attached to the side of the table and pulled down a lever on the case of coiled copper. Slowly and steadily a band of pure energy became visible and hovered in the air, encircling the table the three were sitting at.

'Ready,' Mrs Tavistock said to Tasmin.

'Ready,' said Tasmin as she placed a matching headset over her elaborate hairdo.

In the space in the centre of the table there appeared a coil of white light, spinning like a top. Gradually it steadied itself until it was upright and humming evenly.

'Hello, hello,' Wendle could hear Tasmin say in his head, but her lips never moved. 'Anaru, are you there?'

'I am,' said another fainter voice, and Wendle realised that the two women had not been joking about talking to someone millions of miles away.

'I have brought the man with the transmitter here. We had no trouble with the signal. Is your Controller Opu there?'

'Opu has had an accident,' Wendle could feel Tasmin tense immediately. 'She was caught in an explosion. I am afraid you will have to deal with me until she has been replaced.'

'But I understood your situation was critical? You told me that you didn't have much time left?'

'Controller Opu was fitting a valve to suppress the energy levels we have left when the explosion occurred. She was successful in making the energy levels inaccessible to the creature if it should return in the near future, but in a short while they must be released again so we can use them. It has merely bought us a little time.'

'I see,' Tasmin mused. 'So you still need to trace the Star Dancer?'

'Of course,' Anaru said. 'But the computer must choose another controller before we can negotiate anything with you. I'm sure you understand that.'

'Oh yes,' Tasmin told her, relieved that they were still in dire danger. 'When will this be?'

'There is much for her to do when selected, but I think it likely you will be given priority. Whatever you do, please keep in the contact zone, and do not move the transmitter.'

'All right. You want to make contact with the young man?'

'Yes.'

'His name is Toby,'

Tasmin reached across to flick a switch on the equipment on his head.

'Toby,' said an alien voice inside his head. 'Can you hear me?'

Wendle froze in every muscle. Anaru kept repeating the name 'Toby' and he felt as though his spirit was being prised from his body. Then his mind suddenly heard the voice of the young man saying,

'I can hear you . . . Stop calling me . . . I cannot move.'

'What is the matter, Toby?' the alien voice went on. 'You must not fight the loop.'

'You must not call me Toby,' the young man protested. 'Toby is not Wendle . . . He cannot come . . .'

'Shut the power down!' snapped Mrs Tavistock, who could tell something was dreadfully wrong. Wendle's eyes were suddenly motionless and his body slumped back in the armchair. 'You've killed him you silly little fool!'

Tasmin instantly closed the equipment down, giving Anaru no clue as to why, and looked at the lifeless body in the armchair. 'That's torn it. What do we tell them now?'

'Interesting,' mused Opu, who had been listening to the conversation outside the loop, on Anaru's transmitter.

'Probably put too much power through him,' Anaru said. 'Seems as though he's dead by the way they behaved. If that's

the case, you won't be raising any Star Dancer without him.'

She was about to shut off the power when Opu called out, 'No. Don't, leave it on.'

'But I can't keep the system open for long. You know it can interfere with other planets if they are using the same frequencies.'

'But didn't you understand?'

Anaru gave her a blank look.

'That man insisted his name was not Toby. He may have originally been Toby, who should have died one of their centuries ago, but that interfering machine gave him longevity.'

'So?'

'So it is possible his mind was not able to stand the strain of it, unlike the other three, and it gradually began to reject his body. Although his body went on living, his spirit refused to accept the idea and tried to claim back his personality. Toby had probably begun to reject immortality years before, but was tied to it in the absence of death.'

Slowly Anaru's face lit up. 'Because I kept calling his name, it was just enough to make his spirit break out of his body. So, although Wendle's dead, Toby's spirit could still be around. It had so much knowledge about what was going on it may not immediately return to the evolutionary spiral.'

'It may be here with us, or waiting on Perimeter 84926 for us to call it again. And if we can contact it, it may just be able to tell us what this Star Dancer is.'

Anaru did not even waste time in replying. She disconnected the link to Healphani who had been listening in, and increased the power to the chamber where Tasmin and Mrs Tavistock were still sitting. The two women had to dive beneath the table to escape the scouring surge of power which briefly swept about the room in an explosion of light. In an instant it was gone, and so was Wendle's body.

12

Gabrielle stepped from the train and passed through the white picket fence of the rural station on to a gently sloping path which led to the inviting lake she had seen on the map. As she walked she pulled a library book from her shoulder bag and glanced through it, seeming to wend her way instinctively down the twisting pavement without needing to look up. Passing a couple of large Victorian houses and their monkey puzzle trees, she crossed the narrow road and was standing right next to the cool expanse of water. Unlike the sea, it lay calm and dark green, spangled with a profusion of pastel water lilies. The only movement in the water was caused by the flow from a weir beneath a bridge on the far side.

Gabrielle stood under the branches of a willow for a moment. It was cool under the lacy curtain of leaves and she turned lazily to see who was making the rapid footsteps so out of place in the quiet village. It was certainly no tourist. He was dressed in a navy blue suit and trenchcoat, and his dark face and hair were easily recognisable. She retreated further behind the willow's concealing curtain and wondered at the coincidence that had brought Weatherby and herself to the same unlikely place at the same time.

Gabrielle was tempted to dash out and surprise him in the same way that he had nearly frightened the life out of her on two occasions, but something instinctively told her not to. If Weatherby was here, then it was more than likely Wendle was as well. Without moving, she watched him make his way rapidly to one of the large houses. He did not seem to want to go inside right away and, after nosing about for a few minutes, disappeared round the back of the place. Gabrielle sank to the carpet of soft grass beneath the willow, and

smiled wryly to herself at the coincidence. But as her surprise slowly wore off, other thoughts and questions began to crowd her mind. What if it had not been a coincidence? Toby had led her to Wendle on other occasions. What if some other agent were doing the same thing now?

This thought momentarily took her aback. It was as though her argument were suggesting that she was being attracted by the transmitter. What on earth could she have in common with the mysterious Star Dancer which had arrived and departed so conveniently, so destructively? True, it had rescued Wendle, Weatherby and herself from a very unpleasant situation as though it had logic of its own, and something had managed to weaken gratings and unbolt doors so she could find out where Wendle was. It seemed as though the Star Dancer might have been following her about as well as Wendle. Then all at once her blood seemed to lose its heat. A thought so dreadful had crossed her mind that she let out an audible gasp of horror.

Gabrielle glanced rapidly about as though searching for evidence. All she could see immediately were the willow branches concealing her. She allowed herself to relax totally and, with great dificulty, managed to clear her brain of all her tumbling thoughts. There was no breeze, and the long strips of leaves hung motionless before her. Very lightly, as though gathered up by invisible threads, the curtains of willow were drawn gently aside. Automatically, she rose and walked through the space. They fell back into position again.

She had an answer of a kind. An answer more difficult to believe than the story Wendle had told her about meeting a machine from another world. It would explain why she could never remember her nightmares, and why Wendle wanted her to go away before the Kybion could trace her. And what would happen if the Kybion did manage to catch up with her? A shudder ran down her spine, but she realised that if she had as much power as she suspected it was unlikely the machine would be able to do anything.

Gabrielle walked alongside the lake, pondering. Just to

make sure she was not having nightmares then and there, she lifted the occasional water lily from the lake with her mental energy, then let it drop back down again. As she did so, the birds suddenly stopped singing to their chosen mates. Something grey and small fled so rapidly at her approach she was unable to tell what it was.

So she was the Star Dancer; the answer was simple, but incredible. With the energy she had stolen in her spirit form from this other planet, the potential power she possessed far exceeded her mental capacity to control it. But she knew she would have to try. Gabrielle could not bear thinking about the damage she was about to cause the other planet and the fact that Toby had been living in his cage of longevity for so long, waiting for her to turn up.

Her mind still baulked at the horrific awareness though. Suddenly Gabrielle was pacing her own respiration as though fearful of breathing out flames. With half a dozen airline tickets she could stop as many wars . . . or more likely start them. What if she sneezed and the airliner blew up? Could she fly away, or save the other passengers? Given the power craved by the human race ever since it discovered it had a thumb that could oppose its fingers, Gabrielle was painfully aware she hadn't the faintest idea what to do with it. She had to give it back. In heart and mind she was no Shiva. Some would have revelled in the ability to destroy worlds, but she found the awareness bleakly tranquillising. Apart from that, she had never been so confused in her life.

Gabrielle compelled herself to do a complete circuit of the lake before arriving at any decision. She was only too aware of what could happen if she failed in any solution she settled on. She was again standing by the willow tree when the intangible something which had been attracting her to the place was suddenly no longer there. Perhaps the transmitter had malfunctioned or Wendle had been killed? But no, in the same moment she had missed it, she was sure it was transmitting again, but in what direction she was unable to tell.

Gabrielle realised she could delay no longer. She must somehow learn to leave her body as Toby had done. She returned to the shade of the willow and sat propped up against its trunk. Clearing her mind, she concentrated on Toby. Through her half-closed lids she saw a faint shape moving with the sunbeams dancing through the lattice of leaves. Unable to bring it into focus, Gabrielle closed her eyes completely, and there before her was Toby in his Victorian costume, more distinct than she had ever seen him before. He raised his thin hands, covered by the frilled cuffs of his cream shirt, and beckoned her to rise. It was difficult at first, but the more she relaxed, the freer her consciousness seemed to be of her body. She rose to join him and looked back at her sleeping shape beneath the willow tree. She had done it. But Toby suddenly started to grow fainter as though he were being dragged away. She tried to follow him, but his spirit seemed to be passing from one spiritual plane into another. It was then that she suspected that Wendle had died and Toby was no longer bound to his mortal body.

Gabrielle felt a sense of relief. At long last he had been released from the existence he so hated. It was now up to her to find and somehow rectify the damage her marauding spirit had been doing. She picked up the signal of the transmitter, but it was far away. She knew she must trust her monstrous subconscious to lead her conscious thoughts to the planet.

The journey started gently enough, albeit faster than the speed of light. But thought was the determining factor in this journey. As she hovered to wonder at Saturn and its myriad rings, her attention was suddenly snatched into deep space. Gabrielle gave herself time to wonder if she was still in the same universe. But the signal was still there. Having made her first mistake, she decided to take a tighter grip on the reins and not let her subconscious bolt again.

Cautiously Gabrielle followed the path through the worlds and suns that her spirit seemed used to taking. Much to her irritation it hovered and weaved through the more spectacular places at a leisurely rate, and there was nothing she

could do to hurry it on. One instant she felt herself flapping about like a butterfly through a porridge of semi-solid gases, and the next soaring through the solar wind of a crimson sun in a ball of glowing white fire. She began to wonder what had produced these flights of fancy in her dream existence.

One place Gabrielle's subsconscious self seemed intrigued by was a huge transparent construction the size of a planet and fashioned like a gyroscope. It spun slowly in its own orbit about a sun, and by the massive engines in its centre, she could tell it was capable of leaving one solar system to go to another whenever the need arose. She meandered about its spacious sparkling decks, made of solid diamond. The walls too had that distinctive crystalline glitter, and through them she could see the imaginative creatures which had built it all, living in the vegetation and environment that suited them best.

Could these creatures be engineers, Gabrielle wondered? It looked as though they were building something in the centre of the gyroscope where the engines were located, and she saw where the main body of the world could be opened to release the construction. But all this wondering was not going to help her find the other planet. She tried to jar her dawdling subconscious into remembering where it was heading, but it was no good.

Perhaps her body's experience of time was not relevant to time as her spirit knew it. Perhaps if her aware mind had rushed her spirit to its destination she would arrive at exactly the same time as if she had let her subconscious make the journey its own way. The mortal mind must be a very limited thing when it came to perspective; still, she felt anxious about arriving in time to save the Ojalie from dwindling out of existence.

As the familiar signal became stronger and stronger, Gabrielle found herself flitting through a pink sunset of flying creatures on another planet. They were all hurrying to find a space on high ground, and did not notice her descent to a hotch potch collection of round buildings, somehow manag-

ing to cling to each other. Gabrielle was aware that she was becoming visible as a signal from one of the lower structures summoned her to enter through a curtain of coloured light beams.

Suddenly she understood the history of this strange world: its formation, its suns, its ancient beliefs and modern hedonism. In every Ojalie's mind there was already a name for her . . . Vian Solran, Star Dancer. They believed her to be the deity born from a primeval quasar . . . devourer of stars, disrupter of the galaxy, and menace in general. Gabrielle had to correct their misconceptions about that. Behind the light beam curtain sat the only Ojalie she could make contact with. She had to enter that round room.

Two dumpy figures with large skulls and expanded wings were inside, their glowing orange eyes gazing intently at something lying before them in the centre of a circle. Gabrielle moved into the invigorating energy flowing round the circle and looked down with them. On the floor, in the centre of a pile of dust, lay a small blinking sphere. As she came closer it seemed to be winking at her. She realised she was looking at the transmitter Wendle had been carrying inside him for so many years.

13

The result of Anaru's spontaneous experiment which had sent a beam of energy across the galaxy to scour the room where Tasmin, Mrs Tavistock and Wendle sat was a shock. Instead of dragging Toby's spirit to join them in the loop, a crumpled body suddenly appeared in their circle of energy.

'You must have used too much power!' Opu called out.

'It's just as well he was already dead.' Anaru caught her breath and looked down at Wendle's rapidly disintegrating body. 'Our atmosphere would have killed him instantly anyway. We'd better make sure Annac never finds out about this or she'll think we've been using the Kybini System on living tissue. That would make her mad, especially as she never managed to work out how it could be done.'

'I think that could be the least of our worries.'

'What now?' asked Opu, not anticipating anything worse than impending annihilation.

'Apparently something the human had was a little more resilient. Look.' Anaru pointed to the pile of dust where Wendle's remains had been a split second before.

There sat the small blinking sphere he had been carrying for over a century.

'Now we have the transmitter,' Opu observed in very flat tones. 'That was not quite what I had in mind.'

'Perhaps we could use the Kybini System to transport it somewhere else before the Star Dancer turns up?'

'Not a chance. There won't be time, I expect, and we have to make contact with the thing anyway.'

'I'm not too keen on sitting in the same room with it. I have been hardened to most things over the years, but sudden incineration has not been one of them.'

'You'd better leave and tell control what has happened.'

'I can't do that,' Anaru protested. 'You're not a seer and could never handle this equipment. And as something is liable to visit us at any second, we may need it.'

'What's the chance of us still communicating with it through the loop?'

'There isn't a chance at close range. Our only chance is if it wants to communicate with us. I'll keep the power on and hope it accepts the invitation, but we must both leave the loop.' Reluctantly Opu obeyed.

'How long?'

'Impossible to say. Spirits of any sort do not have the same sense of time we do.' Anaru told her. 'It could already be here.'

'So you reckon it is a spirit?'

'I daren't think of it being anything else at the moment. At least we would stand a chance of meeting something with a limited intellect, as opposed to a steaming mass of energy.'

'Well, here's hoping . . .' Opu stretched her wings to wait.

Shortly afterwards the dust that had once been Wendle's body began to scatter gently as a pillar of energy stood within the loop, drinking the power from Anaru's equipment.

'It *is* a spirit,' Anaru whispered. 'I can sense it.'

'Well, let's hope it's friendly,' Opu muttered into her beak as some semblance of a shape appeared in the middle of the dangerously close energy source.

'It looks like a human.' Anaru was too stunned to ask it to confirm her suspicion.

'They can's be that backward if they can do this, then.' Opu looked up at the small-skulled creature perched on top of legs that seemed to her perilously long. She was tempted to reach out and touch the transparent glowing form.

'Don't do that! There's enough power there to incinerate this side of the city.'

Opu pulled back quickly, wondering how she could have been so idiotic. The strange long-limbed creature with streaming hair and swirling ribbons of energy was so

fascinating she almost forgot Ojal's survival was dependent on her wits.

'What do you want here?' Anaru was compelled to ask, as Opu was taking time to collect her senses. If the creature understood she was trying to contact it, it made no sign.

'Do you know what you are doing to our planet?' Opu suddenly demanded as her presence of mind returned. 'Are you here in your natural form, and do you understand what we are saying?'

The Star Dancer remained motionless and did not even look down at them.

'Perhaps we can only talk to it through the loop?' Opu said, about to re-enter the circle.

'Don't be so idiotic!' shrieked Anaru. 'This is pure energy. It will carbonise you in seconds.'

'But we have to contact it. It must have intellect of some sort.'

'You cannot go into the loop. Just keep talking to it.'

'It's no use. It's probably only here because the transmitter brought it. It may not even be aware of our existence.' Opu turned back to the Star Dancer. 'If you can't make contact, but understand us, try to give us a sign.'

'What sign?' asked Anaru.

'Don't interfere.' Anaru was only too pleased to be let off the hook and kept quiet. 'Can't you wave or something . . .? Stop looking at that wretched transmitter for a second . . . All right then,' Opu sighed. 'I'll smash it if that's what you want.'

'Suicidal fool!' squawked Anaru.

'Shut up. We have to make contact somehow before it becomes bored and loses interest in the transmitter. This is probably the only chance we have.' She looked intently at the Star Dancer. 'I am going to reach out and smash the transmitter. If you understand me, go to the nearest refractor station. If you do not understand me and don't leave the loop I'll be killed as soon as I break into it to touch it.'

'No, Opu. It's not worth the risk.'

'There is no other way. If it fails you must contact main control immediately and let them know what has happened.'

'I don't like it,' Anaru protested, but Opu was already tensing herself to reach out and strike at the transmitter.

Her orange eyes glowing with the reflection of the Star Dancer's energy, she took a deep breath and plunged her hand through the barrier of the loop.

When she came to she felt as though the ancient buildings above had fallen on her. Gradually she became aware of a more localised pain in her throbbing hand. Anaru had shut the loop down and was swiftly pulling a fragment of the transmitter out of her palm.

'It's gone,' Anaru said.

'How long?' asked Opu.

'Seconds ago. As soon as you touched the loop and were knocked out it left before anything worse could happen.'

'Then it understood. It must be at the station.'

'You can't fly in that condition.'

'Well I doubt if it'll wait for me to walk there, and you know what the shuttle service is like in the old sector.' Opu staggered to the balcony and flapped her wings to make sure they were still operational.

'Be careful . . .' she heard Anaru call as she leaped into the sky of the newly rising yellow sun.

Opu flapped as fast as she dared towards the refractor station. The gathering sunbathers below looked up and wondered whether the strain of everything had eventually become too much for the Chief Controller and she had turned suicidal. The shields of the refractor station were slowly opening. Hanging menacingly above them Opu could see the Star Dancer. Exhausted from the flight Opu dropped on to the control room balcony and staggered into the room. Without explanation she moved the operator at the main console aside and seized the lever which opened the energy pool to the other stations. As she pushed it home, cries of anguish echoed around the control room as though she had just signed everyone's death warrant. 'It'll drink the whole

system dry . . . She's taken leave of her senses . . . Can't somebody shut the shields?' a chorus arose.

Opu locked the lever in position. 'If somebody shuts the shields all the energy we have lost from the pools will spill over the countryside and city and cremate everyone out there,' she said.

'But . . .' whimpered one bewildered voice.

'Watch, will you, just watch.' The staff cautiously lined the wide control room window to look up at the mass of energy still hovering above the open shields.

The Star Dancer had dispensed with its human form. It slowly rotated and seemed to be growing larger and larger. The staff in the control room began to murmur apprehensively among themselves as it expanded so far it practically covered the massive pool which the shields had left unguarded. By the time it had finished growing and hung in the sky like a third sun, all the sunbathers in the vicinity had gone, as swiftly as they could. The Star Dancer began to pulsate slowly, then faster and faster, until it was a shimmering sphere. Gradually a coil of energy spiralled down to dip into the energy pool below. The control room staff, thinking it was only a matter of seconds before it drank the pool dry, could not understand why the power level did not move.

Then they stared in wonderment the needle erratically began to flicker into life. The level slowly but surely rose. The great ball of energy ouside grew smaller and smaller. All the stations which were still operational were being brought back to their normal capacity but, by the time the energy-giving transfusion was over, the Star Dancer was just a speck of light twinkling in the yellow sun's rays.

It was then Opu's knees gave way, her body folded up, and she collapsed to the floor.

'Why didn't you tell me what was going on?' Opu could hear Annac's gruff tones complaining as she gained the balcony of

her home. 'You could've been killed you know.'

'I nearly was on several occasions,' Opu sat up slowly to reply. 'I feel as though I've been drinking neat sunlight from the energy pool. My inside must be like a condemned zone.'

'Serves you right,' snapped Annac, then suddenly found someone else standing beside her on the narrow balcony. 'Who are you?' she demanded.

'I'm Opu's gene partner,' was the breezy reply, and an untidy bundle of something beneath her arm squawked in agreement.

'Good grief,' said Annac, looking down at the wriggling creature. 'Is that what you managed between you then?'

'Well, Opuna's more hers than mine,' Anapa laughed thankfully. 'She's been worrying me to bring her back ever since she left home.'

'And you brought her as soon as it was possible of course,' Opu glowered.

'Well, everyone kept telling me how cruel it was to keep you two apart once the emergency was over.'

Annac smiled to herself. The prospect of Opu now having to look after her horrible child again more than compensated for having been kept out of her confidence. She turned and fluttered unsurely off to the peace of her own home.

14

The beam of energy that had swept through the room where Mrs Tavistock and Tasmin had been transmitting their messages to Anaru left as suddenly as it had come. The two nurses who had attended Wendle took fright and fled for their lives. 'Toby's gone!' shrieked Tasmin, more in fright at his disappearance than in remorse.

'I can see that, you silly little fool!' Mrs Tavistock snapped back. 'They must have tricked us.'

'I knew it was wrong to try and tamper with creatures millions of years more advanced than us,' Tasmin whined.

'Don't be such a silly minx,' scolded Mrs Tavistock. 'Toby was dead anyway. Now they have the transmitter, they also no doubt have the creature that has been draining their planet of energy, and I'm sure that's going to do them a lot of good.'

'Oh . . .' sniggered Tasmin, then started to giggle, 'That'll make things even worse for them won't it . . .' Her mirth stopped abruptly as she noticed an unannounced visitor standing in the doorway.

'May I join in the joke, ladies?' Weatherby enquired, as though inviting himself to a tea party.

'What are you doing here?' demanded Mrs Tavistock.

'I took the liberty of coming in as your other two companions were leaving,' he beamed. 'They seemed quite upset by something, so I thought I would just pop in to see if everything was all right.'

'Like hell you did. You were snooping. I knew you would be back sometime or other.'

'Now why is everyone so suspicious of me?' asked Weatherby with an air of offended innocence that would not have fooled a four-year-old. He looked over the strange

equipment. 'Something scorch the top of your head, Mrs T?' He looked down at the singed cap she was wearing. 'I wonder what could have done that?'

'Why don't you go away? We've told you everything we know about Mr Gunn.'

'But it isn't Mr Gunn I'm after this time.'

'Who then?' demanded Tasmin, unable to hide her guilt. 'Who else could we know anything about?' She could not avoid sending a worried glance towards the leather chair where Wendle had been sitting only minutes before.

'Fair-haired fellow, not very tall . . .' Weatherby added pointedly, 'Age unknown.'

'What do you mean, age unknown?' asked Mrs Tavistock frostily.

'Well, ladies . . . He was rather like you in many ways. For some reason it was very difficult to find out when he was born. And what I did find out seems to suggest he must have been a hundred and twenty-seven years old, about the same age as the "young" lady here. Now there's no law against living for as long as you like, I'm pretty sure, but as Mr Gunn seemed to have the same problem it brought me round to thinking that you all must have been connected in some way more binding than passing acquaintance.'

'Congratulations, Mr Weatherby.' Mrs Tavistock carefully pulled a derringer from her gown under cover of the table.

'Congratulations, Mrs T?' inquired Weatherby.

'Congratulations because you had managed to convince me you were quite a fool. What else do you know?'

'I know that after Mr Gunn had finished with him, Mr Wendle was in a pretty poor state, and though I wouldn't accuse you two ladies of being so heavy-handed, I do know he arrived here yesterday, and in his delicate condition might easily come to some harm without proper attention.'

'What harm?' Tasmin tried to ask as though amazed at his suggestion.

'Now, now, ladies,' sighed Weatherby. 'Where is Mr

Wendle? I'm sure we can't keep this conversation up forever.'

'All right Mr Weatherby,' Mrs Tavistock suddenly smiled. 'Please sit down, and we will try to explain.' She indicated the chair Wendle had been sitting in, much to the barely suppressed concern of Tasmin. 'You may pass me the head piece.'

Weatherby strode nonchalantly to the leather armchair and picked the headset out of its seat. He handed it to Mrs Tavistock and sat down.

'Thank you,' said Mrs Tavistock with one of her off-putting creased smiles. 'Now what I am going to tell you, you may find difficult to believe, so just make sure you listen to it right through to the end. Tasmin is going to fit something on you so you can't move.' She produced the derringer and pointed it at his head. 'So don't move!' Weatherby pouted in complaint but remained still while Tasmin took two leads and wound each of them round his wrists, securing them tightly.

'You are no doubt aware of the current that can run through those leads by looking at this equipment: you're obviously not the buffoon you have been trying to make out you are, Mr Weatherby,' Mrs Tavistock warned him. 'So don't try doing anything that would make Tasmin pull that lever.'

'This is going to be quite a long story by the sound of it, Mrs T. Are you sure you want to keep pointing that pistol at my head all the way through?'

'I am going to be as brief as possible.'

'Good, I wouldn't like to keep you ladies from your tea and vitamin pills.'

'Shut up and listen,' Mrs Tavistock said so forcefully he obeyed. 'Over a century ago, Tasmin, myself, a Mr Humbert and Toby Wendle were escaping from a ship foundering in the Channel, when we were washed into a cavern concealed in the cliffs. We were exploring this cavern when a machine appeared and told us we all had to die, else we would disrupt time by not dying when we should have done. Then it

100

changed its mind and decided it would use Toby Wendle by fitting him with a transmitter that would . . .'

'Attract a powerful energy source which had been taking trips to a planet on the other side of the galaxy where it was sucking dry the energy pools the inhabitants lived on?' Weatherby interrupted.

'How did you know that?' Mrs Tavistock demanded menacingly.

'Toby Wendle must have told him,' panicked Tasmin.

'Shut up, girl, and keep your hand on that lever.'

'No' hummed Weatherby. 'No one told me, not even poor Mr Wendle.'

'Poor Mr Wendle?'

'You killed him, didn't you? You thought you would be clever and try to grab all that power for yourselves, but forgot Toby was never tied to this world in the same greedy materialistic way you are. He didn't want to go on living forever like a mouldering vegetable, and so he got out as soon as he had the chance.'

'How do you know all that if he didn't tell you?' shrieked Tasmin.

'How do you think?' Weatherby asked innocently. He beamed a smile at them that was far from his usual inoffensive and amiable one.

Mrs Tavistock swayed where she sat for a second, trying to take in what he was saying.

'It's impossible. We removed the markers. You couldn't have traced us so easily.' She raised the derringer and fired its two shots at point blank range into Weatherby's chest.

Weatherby did not even flinch. When the smoke from the pistol had dispersed, he looked down at his chest and blew the pulverised remains of the bullets away from his satin waistcoat. His own energy field had stopped them from even penetrating the cloth.

'It's the Kybion . . .' Tasmin whimpered, then in desperation pulled the lever, to circulate a massive number of volts through his body. A halo of energy rose into the air and,

descended to join the terminals attached to Weatherby's wrists so that his body was saturated in electricity. It seemed to be having no effect, and Tasmin resolutely kept forcing the lever down harder and harder.

'Switch it off!' Mrs Tavistock screamed, but Tasmin was deafened by the noise of the equipment and too panicked to heed her.

The coils inside the transparent case started to spark against each other and searing flames shot through the container, melting it. Still Weatherby sat there, impassively watching the two women gradually lose control, screaming ribbons of abuse at each other.

With his wrists still attached to the terminals, he lifted a hand to reach inside his waistcoat. Seconds later the two women froze and gazed disbelievingly at each other across the table. Each could see the other's skin shrinking back to the contours of the skull. The creases and wrinkles that had been there before became folds in the living flesh. Tasmin's make-up was dragged into grotesque lines over her features, and Mrs Tavistock's face crumpled like a mouldy orange as the two women shrank inside their clothes.

Tasmin held resolutely on to the lever and the equipment began to overload. Flames cascaded from the molten remains of the transparent casing and licked greedily at the plaster decoration on the ceiling. The current passing round the table reached a peak of intensity and exploded into a fireball which engulfed the three of them. Flames exploded through the ceiling and soon the building was engulfed in fire.

This time the fire brigade managed to send a full attendance in twenty minutes, but twenty minutes was a long time for a greedy fire to be left to its own devices. The local residents turned out in force to see the conflagration. Many left their jobs, either in shops or picking the strawberries in the fields.

'Must've been burning those ruddy candles again,' an old man said to the stranger in a trenchcoat standing beside him.

'That so?'

'Yes,' the old man went on, convinced of his facts. 'That weird old bird and her friend were always up to something odd. You could see them lights flickering through the windows at night as though it were Christmas.'

'Odd,' joined in a middle-aged woman. 'Those two were odd all right, and I'm not so sure about the other pair who dashed off to the railway station not so long before this happened.'

'What pair?' demanded Weatherby.

'Looked like nurses. The old girl always looked pretty sick to me. Wouldn't be surprised if they didn't have something to do with it.'

'Really?' enquired Weatherby so pointedly that the woman understood.

'Are you a policeman?'

Weatherby produced his identification from an embroidered waistcoat pocket. The woman glanced at it, and the old man seized hold of his wrist to pull his hand closer for a better look.

''Struth,' he exclaimed as he touched Weatherby's metal watch strap. 'You feel as though you're on fire as well.'

'I have a very warm disposition,' Weatherby explained impassively as he replaced the card. 'Small children and animals think I'm marvellous. It's only adults who don't care for me much.'

'Don't suppose you have to arrest many small children and animals, do you?' laughed the old man, putting the heat of the watch strap down to his own ageing sense of touch. 'You want us to make some sort of statement then?'

'It seems you could be very helpful in assisting us with our investigations. So if you wouldn't mind . . .?' At those words Weatherby turned to see a queue of local residents waiting to offer statements as well. The fire had effectively gutted the building and the firefighters were paddling about in the remains, so it seemed as though he was going to be the next attraction.

15

As pins and needles shot through her hands and arms, Gabrielle twitched herself awake to look at the curtain of willow leaves surrounding her. The now familiar smell of smouldering wood met her nostrils as she came round. Water from firefighters' hoses was trickling down the bank and into the lake. Before she could pull herself up to part the curtain and look out to see what had happened an amiable voice said soothingly, 'Feeling all right?'

Gabrielle jerked round to see Weatherby sitting under the tree close to her.

'You must have slept well to have missed that,' he smiled. 'Suppose I should be glad you hadn't managed to find your way inside this time.'

'What happened?' She reached out to part the willow and see the remains of the Victorian house. 'That was the place I saw you nosing about some while ago,' she accused him.

'Well, don't blame me.' Weatherby lifted his hands in innocence. 'Apparently the ladies had the habit of playing with candles.'

'Wendle's dead, isn't he?'

'I reckon he must have been inside the building with the other two when it went up,' Weatherby evaded convincingly. 'Fire Officer doesn't think he'll manage to find enough for half an autopsy, but I've got the evidence to prove Wendle was there.'

Gabrielle decided to say no more. He was hardly likely to believe her if she told the truth. It was difficult enough for her to digest. After a pause she asked, 'You didn't think I was in there as well, did you?'

'But you weren't. I don't think I could stand the thought of a young thing like you going up in flames, or coming to any

sort of harm for that matter.'

'You sound as though you really meant that.'

'I do. It was never in me to let anyone come to harm. I don't think like that.'

Although Gabrielle felt as though a tremendous weight had been lifted from her mind, her legs were very unsteady. When she tried to rise, she toppled over as though drunk.

'Steady,' said Weatherby, catching her. 'You must have been fast asleep. I think I'd better take you back in my car.'

'Haven't you got a lot to do after the fire?' Gabrielle asked, though she was grateful for the offer.

'Sure, but it's unlikely those three will be plotting any more insurance frauds, or anything else for that matter, so there's no hurry.'

Gabrielle's thoughts were no longer turbulent. Although quite tired, she felt strangely refreshed.

After Weatherby had seen her back to the cottage she slept soundly until the next morning. She had even been too tired to dream, though she fell asleep thinking about Toby and woke with his image still in her mind. But he had to be at peace at last. Perhaps it was his ghostly way of reminding the Star Dancer to behave itself. Gabrielle was sure she had that under control. She would not have dared sleep at all if she thought otherwise. No . . . thoughts and suspicions still lingered, but it was not a matter she could mull over with someone else. She would have to lay her own ghosts.

It was still early when Gabrielle put on her walking shoes and trudged over the beach towards the village to return her library book and buy some groceries. She resisted the temptation to visit Wendle's bungalow on the way, and arrived just as the library was being opened. As she handed the book back, she apologised with a smile, 'I found it difficult to get into. Things kept distracting me.' Then she selected a volume twice as thick and strode off to the nearest grocer. Inside she met the old lady called Dot.

'What did he say then?' she said.

'Not much,' Gabrielle managed to grin before she went on her way.

This time she was unable to pass the bungalow. She walked down the slope and opened the unlocked door. To her surprise, everything had been tidied up. She could not see how Wendle would have had the opportunity to return to do it, and it was even more unlikely one of the locals was responsible. Even the mugs they had been drinking from had been picked up from the floor, washed, and placed on the draining board.

Gabrielle wandered about the living room looking at everything, but touching nothing. Then, feeling as though she was trespassing, and remembering the first time she had met Wendle when he had told her to go away, she left silently.

In the caverns under the cliffs Weatherby was fiddling with the controls on one of the cavities in the main chamber. Through the transparent wall an image was spluttering into life. Eventually a silver-scaled Taigalian peered accusingly at him from it, before announcing with extreme gravity, 'You are one of the most incompetent androids ever to be designed.'

'Why?' asked Weatherby in less than genuine amazement.

'Why have you waited until the emergency was over before contacting us?'

'What was there to tell you? You never gave me any instructions about having to contact you every few minutes. Besides, I was busy.'

The silver figure decided to try another tack. 'Why didn't you neutralise the energy source as soon as you discovered it?'

'Well, I couldn't kill the young girl, could I? She didn't know what she was doing, and when she did realise she was able to put it right.'

'You did nothing. You are totally useless. You will

dismantle yourself and cease functioning. You cannot even be trusted to collect elementary information about the planet.'

'I can walk under water.'

'That was not intended to be your prime function,' the Taigalian snapped back.

'And I've got a good job in the police force. They might even give me a medal after clearing up those insurance scandals.'

'You were programmed to take the appearance of a human being. You have not been instructed to become one.'

'But I like it. It's comfortable inside this body. Anyway,' Weatherby concluded, 'there's nothing you can do about it.' He switched the picture off and strolled back out of the tunnel, saying to himself as he went, 'Nothing . . . Nothing at all.'

The first moon had reached its meridian and its reflected light bathed the crystal platform on to which glimmering silver bodies had arisen from the foaming green sea. They needed no illumination other than the massive moon as they took their places on the tiers of the platform and waited.

Unlike the warm planet of Ojal with its perpetual sunlight and dense atmosphere, Taigal Rax was a cool, dimly-lit world. Though there was enough daylight to support its life forms, the continents had been submerged by the oceans long ago and most of them were happy beneath the water's surface. The Taigalians carried water in their spacecraft as others carried atmosphere. They had evolved to take their essential gases from both air and water. Once they had been green but, now one of the most sophisticated amphibious species, they had turned silver. As their blood was cool, so was their appearance and manner. Though not uncharitable, they were frighteningly practical.

One of the Taigalians was elevated on a pedestal created from a phosphorescent beam to address them.

'This will not take long,' the speaker told the meeting. 'It is only a minor matter which needs your authorisation.' She went on to explain that their planet had transmitted an android to Perimeter 84926 for the Ojalie, in order to help them trace the Star Dancer. Although designed to the most advanced standards by both planets, the android had not fulfilled its function of neutralising the creature on its planet of origin, had involved four humans with potentially disastrous results, and now refused to dismantle itself when instructed.

'Perhaps you designed it too well?' a voice from the audience suggested.

'Perhaps,' the speaker agreed. 'It was very sophisticated and able to assume any human form it selected, being capable of recalling any knowledge or minor information it would have needed to take in real humans. It even has the ultimate potential of acquiring a human biology while its original material and circuits are slowly absorbed.'

The audience was silent for a moment, and only the wind and crashing of the waves could be heard until another voice enquired, 'Doesn't that mean it could in every respect become a human being, and without us having control over it, do what it wanted?'

'It could. It would contravene all laws on the matter of non-interference that have ever been made. We must have your authorisation to activate the service robots we have in the oceans of Perimeter 84926 to capture and destroy it.'

'Isn't there any other way?'

'The only alternative is to leave it alone, and even if that were not in contravention of so many laws, we have no idea what it would get up to.'

'How powerful is it at the moment?' several asked at once.

'As far as we know it still has the potential built into it as an android. This it may or may not decide to keep. If it wants to assume human form completely, then, naturally, it will not be able to carry those power units. This would make it much easier to catch. As soon as we have captured it, it will be

scanned to discover the reason for its malfunction, then dismantled. For this we must have your authorisation.'

The audience chattered and nodded amongst themselves. Then they plunged into the sea to return to their homes, where they would make their decision. As the beam lowered the speaker to the platform she said to one of her colleagues waiting below, 'There'll be no problem here. Better tell the auto engineers to start the signal. Then we can send the service robots out as soon as we have the authorisation.'

'This is going to be somewhat unpleasant,' the colleague reminded the speaker.

'Stupid machine should have thought of that before. The Watchers would probably dismantle our orbit if they ever found out about this. No one can afford to break laws like these.'

'It might be missed by the humans who know it.'

The speaker did not answer for a moment. Eventually she replied thoughtfully, 'It cannot tell anyone on Perimeter 84926 what it is, and they would not believe it if it did. So it will be a simple matter to pick it up and have it dismembered without arousing any suspicion.

'All that technology. What a waste.'

In the transparent coolness of a station tower far above the water's surface, auto engineers Insac and Helto later received confirmation of the speaker's proposal and activated the signal to the receivers deep in the Earth's ocean.

The operatives had been originally selected for their calm reason, practical execution of duties and inability to wonder at miracles of nature. That was some while ago and they were both mature enough now to wonder why they had applied in the first place, especially Helto. Insac, her regular shift partner, was well aware she would rather be travelling the solar system or piecing together data from deep space probes. In exchange for promising not to make public his liaison with a deep ocean mineral analyst, Helto was

occasionally allowed to air her unTaigalian views without fear of report.

'Only call out two at first,' Insac said. 'It must still be carrying the power units. We don't want to attract too much attention.'

'We don't want to attract any attention,' Helto reminded him. 'Those robots are grotesque. Think how they would appear to a human being.'

'They wouldn't be able to stand the pressure down there if they weren't. It's the only place we can keep them out of their interfering hands.'

'Why can't we wait and see if it really has decided to create a human biology for itself? Then we would know it must eventually die of old age.'

'Because laws are laws,' said Insac. 'We just better make a good job of it and send in the results when we have them. I'll stand by to activate the robots when they are free of their cocoons.'

16

Spending several days recuperating from her odd and traumatic experience, Gabrielle was almost relieved to receive a phone call from Penny to say that she and Paula were coming home early because the weather was so foul. With only a brief visit from Weatherby in that time, Gabrielle felt as though she needed someone to talk to. Her nightmares had left her, but strange dreams had begun to invade her sleep. A faint voice seemed to call her from the abyss of space and she feared one night she might go to it and never be able to wake up again.

Then, one night, the voice became distinct. Gabrielle had just been paying one of her regular visits to the enigmatic artificial world where some vast mysterious device was being constructed. Practically on the verge of discovering what it was, a small thought invaded her dream.

'Why look so hard, Star Dancer?' it asked.

'I gave that name up,' Gabrielle protested before she had time to wonder who was calling her. 'Why shouldn't I be curious?'

'But you already know everything in this universe, my delinquent offspring.'

'Offspring?' Gabrielle's attention was totally broken. 'Who are you?'

'My name is Vian Solran.'

'But . . . you're the monster the Ojalie believe came from the quasar.'

'I also gave up all my bad habits . . .' the thought sighed. 'In fact, I not only gave them up, I became a Watcher.'

'Watcher — that sounds familiar.'

'I am an implement of the Law. I have to hold my power in abeyance until called upon by that worthy institution.'

'Then who makes the Laws of the galaxy?'

'Us Watchers.'

Gabrielle paused.'If you are who you say, why waste time talking to a mere astral traveller like me?' she asked.

There was a gentle ringing laugh.

'You are my thought child. Se who had three parents.'

'Se?'

'You. Thought has no gender.'

'Then you gave me that power . . . but why?'

'So you would live. Your species needs many more like you in their mortal lives.'

'But I nearly destroyed a planet.'

'Some of my offspring can be careless. They inherited that from me.'

'If I hadn't realised . . .'

'You would not have done it. That was why I chose you. Unlike most others, your subconscious had sense as well.'

'But Toby, Gunn, Mrs Tavistock and Tasmin . . .?'

'Mortal concerns. They no longer exist as you knew them,' Vian Solran reassured Gabrielle. 'I'd like you to understand. Come with me.'

The strange mechanical planet faded and millions of symbols snowed about Gabrielle.

'What are these?' she asked.

'They are the Laws.'

The symbols parted like curtains and spiralled away.

'What does a Watcher do then?'

'We watch. Some of us watch a million worlds, some concentrate on those few viruses floating in space which can lay waste to star clusters . . . We watch . . '

'And . . .'

'We seldom do anything. Each of us has the power of a super-nova. Together, it is that of a quasar. Look . . . '

Until then Gabrielle did not know Vian Solran had any form, but she was suddenly aware her guide was pointing to a small figure, apparently fast asleep, in a cushioning web of

mist. It was young, fair, and blissfully unaware of their presence.

'Toby!' exclaimed Gabrielle.

'I have taken per from the life spiral for a short while. You told me se needed to rest.'

'I told you . . .?'

'You tell me many things, Star Dancer. Why shouldn't you? Aren't you my child? Or would you rather see your mortal parents?'

'Where are they?'

'Look . . .'

Suddenly Gabrielle was gazing down from the sky. On the surface of a dry brown landscape many humans swarmed in the dull water of a wide river.

'But that's India!'

'Your father believed he would be reincarnated there after he died. Shall I point him out?'

'No!' Gabrielle suddenly blurted out. 'Show me my mother.'

The Earth disappeared. Thick purple clouds enveloped them. Gabrielle was swimming in the outer layers of a gaseous planet. Swimming with them were kite-winged creatures.

'Shall I point her out?' asked Vian Solran.

'No,' sighed Gabrielle.

'What is wrong?'

'With the power you gave me, I ceased to be any mortal's child.'

'Every mortal and immortal thing is related. Come to me again and I will explain how.'

'When?'

'You will know. Now you must answer the door.'

Gabrielle woke with a start to find the milkwoman wanting to know how many pints she needed.

Gabrielle was ready at the station to help Penny and Paula carry their suitcases down the path to the cottage, and

listened patiently while Penny went into the tedious details of their failed package holiday. The hotel had only been partly built, the water had to be boiled and Paula had somehow managed to get sunburned on the only day it stopped raining.

'You should have a suntan like mine,' Gabrielle teased her. 'You would cook more gradually then.'

'Has everything been all right here?' Penny eventually asked after unburdening her calamities. 'You look very tired. Are you sure you're well?'

'I did have a rather unpleasant surprise.'

Penny was immediately worried. 'Why? What's happened, Gabby?'

'Well . . .' Gabrielle started carefully, knowing she would have to tell her something, but not sure how much. 'A policeman phoned to say he would be popping in later today,' and when Penny's jaw dropped, 'It's all right though. I'm not in trouble of any sort. It's just that I was the last person to see that strange blond man who lived along the cliff before he was killed in a fire.'

'My God!' gasped Penny, and sat down, still clutching the shoe and bottle of eau de Cologne she had been unpacking.

'Did you know him?'

'No . . . no. It's just that nothing's ever happened around here since Albert Cooney ran through the village, wearing only a union jack and a plastic bucket, screaming that Napoleon was coming and it took half a dozen nurses to catch him.'

'Oh, he was killed some way from here,' Gabrielle reassured her. 'I met him on top of the cliff and we got talking. They say apparently he never used to talk to anyone, so I suppose they think he might have told me something they couldn't have found out otherwise.'

'What a thing,' Penny shook her head. 'He was a strange one, I know, but he never did any harm to anyone.' She paused, 'Are you sure everything else is all right?'

'Of course,' Gabrielle laughed. 'As long as you don't mind this detective coming here. He's a bit of a humorist — but

114

really quite nice,' she added, hoping Weatherby would not go and blab out anything more than she had told Penny.

'Well, we'd better tidy up then.' Penny jumped to her feet. 'What time's he coming?'

'Oh, don't rush about because of him,' Gabrielle told her. 'He's not the type to worry about that sort of thing.'

'But I've not had a policeman here since I had to call them out over . . .' She glanced about to make sure Paula was out of the room. 'Frank coming back to cause trouble after the divorce.'

Gabrielle helped Penny unpack and put the things to be laundered into the washing machine. Then she cooked a meal for the three of them, and by the time Weatherby knocked at the cottage door she felt too tired to answer it. She need not have bothered though, Penny was there before anyone else could reach it. Rearranging her light brown hair and snatching off her apron she swung the door open. She was stunned for a second by Weatherby's striking appearance, and wouldn't have spoken if Weatherby hadn't introduced himself.

'Come in, come in . . .' Penny stuttered, suddenly finding her warm smile, and escorted him to the living room where Gabrielle lay sprawled out in an armchair and Paula sat moping in a corner with her sunburn. Gabrielle lifted a hand in salute, and Paula suddenly stopped moping and became interested.

'Mr Weatherby,' Penny said, as though Gabrielle might not recognise him.

'Hello,' Weatherby beamed as Penny scuttled off to the kitchen to bring in the tea tray.

'Hello stranger,' said Gabrielle, bringing a finger to her lips as she righted herself to tell him to be careful how much he said.

'I've brought something you might be interested in.' Weatherby took an envelope from his inside pocket and waved it tantalisingly.

Gabrielle was not sure how to react. She was gradually

becoming convinced the man was a good deal brighter than she had originally given him credit for.

'Come and sit down then.' Instead of going to the armchair she indicated, Weatherby sat at the table and started to tip the contents of the envelope on to it.

'What's that?' asked Gabrielle as she saw a latchkey drop out, and went to the table to join him.

'I got this several day ago. I couldn't say anything about it to you then because I had to contact the solicitor and make sure it was all above board. She's apparently received the same instructions as well though.'

'What is it?' Gabrielle tried to sneak pieces of paper away from him.

'He must have made his mind up about this while you two were — ' Weatherby stopped abruptly as he felt the hot breath of a curious Paula peering over his shoulder.

'Why not just tell me?' Gabrielle pleaded.

'Wendle left you his bungalow.'

Paula leapt into the air and ran to the kitchen shrieking, 'Mum! Mum! Gabby's been left a house!'

Taking the opportunity of her brief absence, Gabrielle hissed across the table to Weatherby, 'They only know I talked to Wendle before he died.'

'All right.' Weatherby gave her one of his more perceptive smiles. 'How are you feeling now?'

'Shattered.'

'I'm not surprised.'

'I'm beginning to dream about creatures called Watchers and symbols called Law.'

'Watchers . . . ?' Before he could say more, Paula returned, with Penny and tea tray in hot pursuit.

'I don't believe it!' Penny exclaimed, thrusting the tray on to the table and nearly concealing the evidence.

'It's true,' Weatherby assured her. 'I've checked with the solicitor. He sent them this deed of gift and a copy to me. The only problem was, it hadn't been witnessed, but it's been authenticated with a specimen signature, and with no one to

contest it, it looks as though you have acquired property.' He saw that Gabrielle's mixed emotions were making it difficult for her to speak. 'He also left you an endowment so you could afford to keep the place, pay the rates et cetera.'

'Is that what he wanted?' Gabrielle asked, unsure what to think.

'It wasn't a condition, but he expressed the wish that you should.'

'But that would be ideal for you, Gabrielle,' Penny joined in. 'Even if you didn't live there all the year round, it would make you independent.'

'And I could come and stay with you,' Paula reminded her.

'Now don't go and turn it down,' Weatherby said, looking straight at her. 'It's what he wanted. He must have thought he owed you something.'

'Silly man . . .' Gabrielle murmured. 'What do you think?'

'Take it,' he said, laying his hand on the back of hers. 'Here's the latchkey. All you need do is go to town and see the solicitor.'

As Weatherby and Gabrielle were involved in their conversation, Penny was absently holding the teapot and watching Weatherby intently. A couple of drops of the scalding fluid fell on to her foot, but she remained transfixed. Eventually, when the teapot became too hot to hold any longer, she asked, 'Tea anyone?'

'Yes, please, Penny,' Gabrielle replied.

'Mr Weatherby?'

'No . . . no thank you. I had one not so long ago. I won't be keeping you any longer anyway.'

'That's all right. I was going into town to collect a few things, but it's a bit late now. I think I'll leave it till tomorrow.'

'I can give you a lift in if you like?' Weatherby offered.

'Could you really?' Penny's face lit up, although she was not sure whether she should accept his offer.

'Can I come too, Mum?' Paula demanded, also fascinated by Weatherby and the chance of a ride in a police car.

117

'No. You stop here with Gabrielle. I won't be long.'

Leaving Gabrielle to watch over the restless ten-year-old with sunburn, Penny and Weatherby made their way into town.

'Are you sure Gabrielle isn't in some sort of trouble?' Penny asked Weatherby anxiously as they got out of the car. 'This business of being left a bungalow seems odd to me.'

'Oh, apparently Mr Wendle had no relatives. There won't be any disputes about its ownership.'

'It was very quick though.'

Weatherby hesitated for a moment, unable to think of anything else that would sound convincing, then suggested, 'Why don't we find somewhere to talk?'

Penny agreed, and they had no trouble finding a quiet corner tea shop.

'I owed Mr Wendle a small favour and agreed to be his executor some while ago. Gabrielle just happened to be the last person to see him alive,' Weatherby assured Penny over the chrome silver tea service and wheatmeal biscuits, 'We think he may have been murdered, but she's not implicated in any way.'

'Or in any sort of danger?' asked Penny.

'No, goodness no.'

'Only it's that I don't want to worry her foster parents about anything. My brother and his wife have always been very fond of Gabrielle, and it would break their hearts if anything happened to her. She's such a gentle and bright girl, and we all think the world of her.'

Weatherby successfully hid his surprise that they did not seem to know how tough she really was.

'Yes, she does seem like a very bright girl. Perhaps Mr Wendle wanted to give her the opportunity to do things she might not have otherwise been able to?'

'That might be true. Jack and Connie never have been well off since the railways made him redundant two years ago — though they were going to let her go to college if she wanted. But she needs to know the results of her exams first before

deciding.' Penny smiled. 'I am really glad for her, Mr Weatherby. Gabrielle deserves to have a decent chance. She's the only one in the family with any brains. I sometimes think my Paula is going to end up in a shoe shop or as a clerk in the town hall with me.'

Weatherby laughed. Penny's bright eyes could not conceal her glumness at the prospect, and he reassured her, 'Well, she's only young yet.'

At that Penny burst into laughter and half the tea shop turned to see what the joke was.

'At my age, Mr Weatherby,' she managed to say in a whisper as she realised the attention she had attracted, 'I'm forty-four and divorced.' Weatherby shrugged at his mistake. 'How old did you think I was?'

'Much younger than me,' he grinned in embarrassment.

'How old are you, then?' she asked mischievously.

'Something like that,' he replied secretively.

'Really, Mr Weatherby, fancy being ashamed to admit your age,' she teased, and patted the back of his hand.

At her touch, Weatherby felt all manner of unfamiliar feelings flooding through his highly co-ordinated and sophisticated body. He had thought her interesting, but her pretty face framed by brown hair was all that had made her attractive to him at first. Now something alien and unknown was taking hold of his perceptions and he began to worry that he was malfunctioning in some way. Worse still, Penny seemed to be having the same reactions, but he was sure she understood what they were about.

Next day Gabrielle took Paula along the cliffs to show her the bungalow, but did not stay long or let her touch anything. She was still uneasy about it all, and was trying to pluck up the courage to spend a night there.

When they arrived back at the cottage, Penny was just answering the phone. Paula dashed out into the back garden and Gabrielle slumped into an armchair in the living room

and picked up the heavy volume she had borrowed from the library. Flicking through the pages to find the place Paula had lost for her, she could not help overhearing Penny talking to the caller in the hall.

'What do you mean?' she was saying. Yes, I know you're a racist turd, but that still doesn't make it any business of yours . . . Don't be so idiotic. The man's a policeman, so don't think about trying to start trouble!' She slammed the receiver down and marched into the kitchen. Gabrielle momentarily lost interest in her book, and was unable to conceal the wry smile on her face. She decided not to go out for the rest of the day, and waited for the gentle knock at the front door, and Paula's piercing tones shouting, 'Hello, Mr Weatherby. Mum's in the garden and Gabby's in the living room.'

Gabrielle knew it was not her he had come to see. She listened to his footsteps going down the side passage as he found his way into the garden.

Penny tried her best to appear surprised to see him, but hardly succeeded. Although pulling weeds in the garden, she was wearing one of her best dresses and eye make up, which Gabrielle could not recollect her wearing before.

'You left your gloves in the tea shop,' Weatherby said, pulling them from his pocket. 'I was passing so I thought I would drop them in.'

'I didn't think you ever wore them, Mum,' Paula commented in a very loud voice and was promptly told to go and play in the front.

When her bright red shorts and ponytail were out of sight, Penny said, 'That's very kind of you, Mr Weatherby. I'm sure you needn't have bothered.'

'I had some free time. Things are very slack at the moment. It's the time of year you see. With no tourists in these parts and everyone going on holiday . . . things are very quiet,' he said, having for some reason to search his mind for something suitable to say.

'Yes it is . . .' Penny was obviously having the same problem. 'It's not very often we get visitors here.'

The smile faded so suddenly from her face that he had to ask her what the matter was.

Penny stood awkwardly fluttering her hands, as though she did not want to tell him for a moment. Then she blurted out, 'It's my first husband, Frank . . . He saw us together yesterday and jumped to some conclusions.'

'But why worry about that?'

'I had to divorce him because he was so jealous. Even afterwards he used to watch me, until the police stepped in. It was probably only by chance he saw us, but he phoned me this morning to warn me to keep away from you.'

'But he can't do that,' Weatherby laughed. 'He'll be having more trouble with the police if he does that too often.' He put his arm reassuringly round her shoulder, much to the delight of Gabrielle and Paula who were watching from a window.

'But I'm worried, Mr Weatherby. It's not as if you're just any man . . .' She stopped awkwardly, waiting for him to take the point, but for some reason he did not understand the hint, so she went on, 'I mean, he still regards me as his property and never accepted the divorce. I sometimes think he's a little mad.'

'If he gives you any trouble you must phone me right away,' Weatherby released her shoulder to write down two telephone numbers in his notebook. 'This one is the station, and this one my flat.' He tore out the page and handed it to her.

He was about to replace his arm about her shoulder, but glimpsed the grinning faces at the window and changed his mind.

'My Frank always was a bit narrow-minded. In fact he was born believing he was the only one made in the image of God. Once he pulled a knife on a man the same colour as you just because he looked at him the wrong way.' Penny managed to hold his hand without the audience seeing. 'He might try to harm you as well.' Weatherby laughed vigorously at the idea. 'You may be a policeman, but if he's got murder on his mind, that won't stop him.'

'I'm sorry. Seems as though we'd better be careful if we want to meet each other again then.'

'Yes. We had better be careful. There is one thing though.'

'What's that?'

'I'd like to know your Christian name?'

Weatherby was stumped for a moment.

'Well . . .' he hedged. 'My parents weren't Christian.'

17

Assured by the solicitor that Wendle's deed of gift had been genuine, Gabrielle eventually managed to pluck up the courage to stay in the bungalow overnight. She reasoned her fear had been irrational because the only ghost liable to haunt the place would be Toby.

That night, she visited Vian Solran in a nebulous temple at the centre of the galaxy, constructed with the tattered remains of a star shredded by a black hole.

'Why are you here?' Gabrielle asked.

'On the other side of that chasm is my parent, Star Dancer,' said Vian Solran. 'Your grandparent. Wouldn't you like to see per?'

'What . . . ? A black hole?'

'Come with me.'

Vian Solran released the strands of star matter making up the temple and Gabrielle felt herself being pulled down after them. Though she only consisted of thought, she almost panicked at the idea of being unable to return.

'No parent like us would harm their offspring,' the deity reassured her.

With a sudden explosion of light they spun into a dazzling new prospect. Gabrielle turned to see they had been ejected from a quasar.

'Into a black hole, and out of a quasar,' said Vian Solran. 'My parent turned inside out. We can be born as many times as we like.'

'How can a quasar be anyone's parent?'

'Quasars are the parents of us all.'

'But has it intelligence?'

Vian Solran laughed. 'When you're a quasar, you don't need intelligence . . . You are.'

This other universe was young. Its expanse was alight with glowing clouds giving birth to stars. For aeons there would be no night here. Gabrielle may have been a Star Dancer, but this vibrant dimension was too overpowering and she slipped out of her dream sweating with relief.

The next morning Gabrielle dusted the ornaments that were so pleasing to Wendle's orderly mind, and again wondered who could have tidied up the place.

Taking the brief walk into the village, she could not avoid meeting Dot. She knew it would only be a matter of time before she found out she had been left the bungalow, so decided to tell her before the gossips got round to it. Dot was fired with burning curiosity, but could only get Gabrielle to tell her what she had told Penny.

'There's a thing . . .' Dot almost gurgled in joy at getting the news before anyone else. 'I suppose you must know that black man who went in there the other day then?'

Weatherby. Gabrielle laughed at herself for not associating him with the tidy bungalow. Of course he would have had to visit it to search for any clues, and it would have been just like him to have forgotten to lock the door.

'Oh, he's a police detective,' she said, not seeing the harm in letting Dot know. 'He's been investigating the case.'

'Strange fellow he is.'

'He's likeable enough,' Gabrielle found herself defending him. 'He's been pretty good over this business.'

'No, I didn't mean that.'

'What then?' Gabrielle, wondered what was so odd about him that she did not already know.

'One of the lads was setting lobster pots in the cove late the other evening and reckoned he saw him walking along the beach.'

'If you can walk on pebbles without ricking your ankles I don't see the harm in that?'

'But he was in Wrecker's Cove,' Dot told her. 'The only way you can get down is by the sea.'

'He must have found a boat from somewhere or clambered

down somehow,' Gabrielle smiled. 'He's a determined sort of fellow.'

'Not very likely. Though it was still reasonably light he never saw the lad, who was able to watch him walk round the rocks where he had come from and out of sight again.'

Gabrielle suddenly felt uncomfortable. This was something she would have preferred not to know, but having found out so much, asked, 'How far is this cove from the town?'

'Oh . . . not too far, but it's almost impossible to get to over the wasteland. The best way to get into town is to take a bus from the village and go the long way round.'

'But how far do you reckon?'

'Oh,' Dot scratched her chin, 'about a mile and a half as the crow flies.'

'Is that all?' gasped Gabrielle in amazement.

'Can't be any more. There's no coast road because no one much lives along there, only recluses and wealthy boat owners.'

'I never realised the town was that close to the sea,' murmured Gabrielle, though she had practically walked the distance through the tunnel to it.

'Go along there and have look, dear. There's a path at the top of the cliffs. Only don't choose a blowy day or you'll be swept off.'

'I think I will. When's low tide?'

'Couple of hours,' Then Dot warned sternly, 'Now don't you go trying to get down there. The place is a death trap. More people have been lost along that stretch than get parking tickets around here.'

'All right,' agreed Gabrielle. 'I promise.'

Finding it difficult to believe that Weatherby could have found some way out of the underground system to the shore without getting wet, Gabrielle was curious as to how he had got down and later in the morning, she started along the cliff to find out. Even without a wind, the breeze somehow managed to get angrier on the far side of the village and

whistled furiously about the cliffs as though it hated every inch of them.

Gabrielle was relieved when she reached the top of Wrecker's Cove and was able to lie flat and peer over the sheer walls to a semi-circular patch of shingle beach. There was no way down, and no strip of beach connecting the cove at low tide.

The area was desolate, rock strewn and pitted, and probably too unstable to support the foundations of buildings. Beyond a gently rising hill must have been the town. Gabrielle still wanted to believe that there was some simple explanation for Weatherby's apparent ability to walk under water other than the one that kept springing to her mind. It would explain why he had met her inside the caverns that day, how he had managed to walk out of a blazing house and why Wendle had been so anxious she should leave. It did not explain why Weatherby had done nothing to neutralise the power he must have known she had, even though it would have meant killing her. Gabrielle shuddered at the thought. She did not want to believe he was the missing Kybion, especially as Penny had taken such a fancy to him and, impossibly, him to her.

She fought her way back across the cliffs in the teeth of the furious breeze thinking hard all the way.

18

The pebbles rattled and cracked as something of immense weight placed its huge round feet on them as it made its slow way up the shore. Its body was squat and wide. It had several pairs of snake-like arms which it could retract into its body if it did not need them. There was no face in the human sense of the word, but a wide, flat head that joined the shoulders and had a lateral slit running around it.

A light inside the slit flashed and occasionally sent out an intense beam capable of illuminating the darkest corners of the beach in a sickly green light. Its skin was grey and slimy and it left a trail on whatever it touched.

The sea creature was not sure in what direction to take its stroll in the moonlight, and the light inside the slit flashed as though it were searching for something. Then a high frequency sound which excited the neighbourhood's cats and dogs whistled as it tried to locate a brain wave pattern of particular intensity. Having no success, it moved a little further up the shore and repeated the process several times until finally it was standing before a large rambling bungalow which was laid out like a Roman villa. The creature somehow sensed there was nothing substantial enough in its way to prevent it from investigating further and moved into the villa, without opening the door.

It was fortunate the place was empty, because this sea monster hardly had the stealth of a cat burglar. Without a signal it could follow it blundered into pillars and furniture, and eventually achieved the height of bad manners by walking through a wall out into the night air again. Its scanning device evidently did not have the range required and it lumbered back to the waves licking the pebble beach.

Insac and Helto had been watching the pictures sent by the robot from their tower control on Taigal Rax. Turning from the screen Helto concluded, 'Not exactly delicate workers, are they?'

'We'll have to widen its scan. As it'll never be able to run after anything it'll have to be given more calling power,' Insac told her.

'Just as well brain waves are the one thing that can never be changed — though I don't envy the android when that creature gets its tentacles on it.'

'Stop thinking about that,' Insac countered. 'It's not our job to make moral judgements.'

'Then we must be the only ones on this planet without that privilege.' Helto rapidly opened and closed her dorsal fin in annoyance. 'The problem with interfering in other planets' affairs is that there's always containment necessary to protect them from the consequences. Those humans probably wouldn't be affected if we did leave the machine down there.'

'Rules are rules,' Insac reminded her. 'We wouldn't be able to go anywhere if we didn't keep to them. The Watchers would soon deal out the Law. I've never heard of them blasting a planet from its orbit, but it's known it would only take one of them a split second to do it.'

'Then Controller Opu should be taking some of the blame for this as well.'

'Maybe. But we happen to be closer.'

'Oh. I'm going for a swim,' Helto said, stretching her arms and fins.

'Well, remember to close the hatch,' Insac reminded her. 'We don't want the place flooding again.'

'Why not? All that salt's good for you.'

'But it isn't for the equipment. Why do you think they build places this high?'

'So they can touch the stars,' Helto replied, laughing at her serious partner. She opened the hatch to plunge into the cool green depths below.

The Clarke Johnsons were returning late that night from their friends the Rosenbergs to their little villa nestling by the water's edge on a deserted part of the coast. As the car turned into the private road which serviced six other remote bungalows at Heron's Point as well as their own, Mrs Clarke Johnson mentioned that she had one of her foreboding feelings coming on. The Major paid little attention to her as she had been having them regularly every other night for the past twenty-four years. It was not until he drove past the smashed gatepost and saw the massive hole in the masonry in his headlights that he was inclined to believe her.

Being an ex-soldier, he was not going to be intimidated by an intruder, even one that left holes in the sides of bungalows. Despite Mrs Clarke Johnson's many pleas to call the police first, the gallant Major would have burst into his home to take the culprit unawares, but as not only the door had been dismantled, but a good deal of the wall it had been attached to as well, the act would have been somewhat futile.

Once inside he turned on the nearest light switch and saw a series of holes in the floorboards running through the wreckage of their home. They ended at the hole he had seen from the outside of the bungalow. Even he was momentarily staggered and lost his military poise. He was startled by the sound of his wife shrieking, 'Call the police, quickly!'

'Eh—what?' he said, still stunned.

'Oh, never mind,' she said, breaking into a state of sudden calmness when she saw her husband was not going to be much use, promptly making the call herself.

Two whiskies and two gins later, they heard the sound of a police car arriving in their drive.

'What kept you, man?' boomed the irate Major before the police constable and detective could get out of the car.

'Private roads not on maps are difficult to find in the dark, sir,' called Weatherby's voice. 'They need lighting of some sort.'

'I manage all right,' declared the Major with twenty years of military service and a good deal of whisky in his voice. He stared at the tall plain clothes detective in the fancy waistcoat and his pert uniformed companion, who looked as though she had just been transferred from the Girl Guides. 'Is there only the two of you?'

'That's right, sir,' replied Weatherby as he and his teenage colleague bounced and trotted respectively over the fallen front door and masonry that surrounded it. 'But the most efficient available,' he beamed.

The Major's face assumed another stunned expression. 'Me wife.' He jabbed a thumb in the direction of the lady swaying to and fro on a high stool at the cocktail bar. 'She should be in bed, but there's a draught coming through the hole in the bedroom wall.'

'Hole?' asked Weatherby, and the Major pointed his finger towards the end of the trail of destruction.

'Mice around here must be a bit neurotic,' Weatherby observed, but seeing the Major did not have a sense of humour, especially at the moment, he pulled out his notebook. 'When did this happen, sir?'

'Major. Major Clarke Johnson. And I haven't the faintest idea.'

Weatherby caught sight of the slimy trail running along the walls and hall carpet. 'I think we need to call forensic out on this.'

'You can do what you like,' announced Mrs Clarke Johnson swaying completely off the stool and tottering round the holes in the floor to the phone, 'But I am going back to the Rosenbergs for the night.'

'I don't think it would be wise for you to drive in that state, ma'am,' Weatherby warned her, but she was already talking on the phone. 'Call forensic and take Mrs Clarke Johnson wherever she wants, Perkins,' he told the policewoman. He turned to the Major. 'Do you want to go, sir . . . I mean Major?'

'No chance. I want to see what goes on,' he snorted as

though he trusted Weatherby even less that the intruder.

Leaving a couple of sleepy forensic experts to take samples and photographs of anything particularly obnoxious-looking inside the bungalow, Weatherby and his assistant made their way down to the shore.

'Do you believe in sea monsters, Perkins?' he asked.

'I do now, sir,' she replied as she saw the massive indentations in the pebble beach where the shingle had been smashed and impacted. 'You can't pin this one on the mice this time.'

'Doesn't it bother you?' He stopped to measure one of the depressions.

'I would guess from the size and depth of these impressions, that whatever made them would be pretty clumsy,' she mused thoughtfully. 'I think I could easily outrun one of them.'

That logical reply was not the one he had been after. 'They must mean something to you other than elementary mathematics.'

'What's that, sir?' the keen young woman inquired.

'It's all bloody terrifying,' he blurted out so suddenly he surprised himself.

'I never thought of you as the type to get scared, sir. After all, there probably is a quite rational explanation for it.'

'Tell me one, Perkins?' Weatherby pleaded hopefully, becoming aware of an explanation of his own.

'Oh, I'm sure you will be able to work one out,' she smiled sweetly up at him. 'After all, you usually do, don't you?' Then the undersized, over-enthusiastic girl bounded back to the bungalow as another constable waved to her.

Weatherby slumped to the pebble beach and, resting his chin on his knees, flickered his torch idly over the trail of depressions before him. Meeting Penny had kindled one human emotion in him, and now the arrival of this outrageous amount of evidence was fanning another into life. It

was far less comforting and sent a chill of mortal terror through him. He had been over-optimistic in thinking Taigal Rax could do nothing about his opting for android liberation. That slimy something which had lumbered from the depths of the sea had undoubtedly been sent to track him. Jutting out his chin thoughtfully, Weatherby wondered why he was sitting there in full range of it as though he wanted to be carried off and dissected.

He got up and returned to the bungalow and the unfriendly Major.

'Well?' snapped that gentleman as soon as he walked in over the door.

'Oh . . .' said Weatherby absently. 'We'll rehang the door for you, assuming we can find the doorposts, and put a tarpaulin over the hole.'

'I meant, what do you think did it?' the Major bellowed, nearly treading on one of the forensic men collecting specimens from a hole in the floor in his haste to pursue the detective into the living room.

'Well . . .' said Weatherby thoughtfully. 'It's not mice. Whatever came through here wasn't after cheese.'

'You, sir,' barked the Major, 'Are a fool! It no doubt goes with your complexion.'

Weatherby rubbed his smooth chin throughtfully. 'But then,' he mused, 'it might have been a rat.'

19

The next morning Weatherby was inside the cavern under the cliffs trying to raise Taigal Rax on the screen where he had spoken to them before. It was a little more difficult this time. It seemed as though they did not want to talk to him any more, and when something eventually spluttered on to the screen the picture did not come into focus, though an irate voice could be clearly heard.

'This channel should be closed,' it snapped. 'Transmission must cease.'

'But I've got to talk to someone,' Weatherby insisted. 'You can't all have seaweed in your ears.'

'The decision has been made. Nothing will be acknowledged on this channel from now on.'

'No wait — ' Weatherby called before the voice and faint image could disappear. 'Couldn't we come to some arrangement?'

'I do not have the power to make agreements.' And the transmission went dead.

Weatherby left the channel open in the desperate hope that someone would relent and, after several minutes, his wishes were answered. This time there was a distinct picture of a shimmering individual with white-edged silver scales.

'Hello, little android,' Helto said as she watched Weatherby's dejected expression on her own monitor. 'Why are you trying to contact us now?'

'I saw the mess one of your service robots made of a bungalow,' Weatherby told her. 'And I've been thinking about the sort of mess it's capable of making when it catches me.'

'But you had the chance to dismantle yourself. You still could if you haven't decided to develop a human biology.'

From Weatherby's silence she could tell he had. 'When did you make that decision?'

'I met an attractive woman . . .' Weatherby started to explain, but thought better of it.

'You can't fall in love with a human.'

'Well, I just did. Ask the ones who designed me whether it's possible or not. My power units will soon be absorbed and I will be as human as she is.'

'You didn't really think you would be allowed to do that, did you?' Helto asked eventually.

'I didn't think you'd get so touchy about it if I did.'

'Stop the process before it goes too far and dismantle yourself.'

'But I don't want to. Why should I?'

'Because one way or another you will have to be destroyed. That's the Law. I would rather you did it your way.' Helto explained. 'Please be sensible. I know you were constructed to have rational thoughts, even though it seems you haven't used them up to now. You know that we would have to do an internal scan to find out for the engineers what went wrong, and that could be very unpleasant for something as sophisticated as you.'

'Well, how could I be constructed to destroy an energy source without having the ability to kill the being possessing it?' Weatherby demanded. 'Was that rational?'

Helto had to stop for a moment. She was beginning to wish she had not decided to answer the transmission after all. Eventually she replied, 'Please do as I say, it would be terrible if the service robots had to fetch you.' And before Weatherby could reply, the screen went dead.

Weatherby sank to the floor in a kneeling position and rocked backwards and forwards in deep thought. He knew the screen was really dead this time, and probably so was he. He became so wrapped up in his own despondency that he nearly jumped out of his skin when a familiar voice asked, 'Weatherby . . . How could you?'

He spun round in surprise to see an angry Gabrielle looking down at him.

'Touché,' was all he managed to comment at her success in giving him such a fright.

'How could you deceive poor Penny like that?' Gabrielle demanded, obviously not having been able to understand a word of the language he had been using. Weatherby looked up at Gabrielle and knew it would be useless to try and bluff his way out of her suspicions.

'I like being a living thing. I wouldn't deceive Penny for anything.'

'Then you're a muddle-minded machine with a mortality fixation. You can't fall in love with a human.'

'She hasn't told me the attraction is mutual.'

'Well, of course it is. She wouldn't have spent so much time with you over the last few days if it wasn't. Haven't you any sense at all? Why couldn't you have done something useful, like raking the Goodwin Sands level, or skimming up a couple of oil slicks?'

Weatherby could tell by Gabrielle's expression it would only make things worse to reiterate that he loved Penny, so he confessed instead, 'My circuits were designed in such a way that they are capable of developing into living tissue if so instructed . . . that's what I instructed them to do. Soon all my power units and circuits will be absorbed and I will become as human as you are.'

'How could you?' demanded Gabrielle. 'I was never an android.'

'No, you became a Star Dancer instead.'

'I didn't choose to.'

'I didn't choose to be an android. I wouldn't have needed to be an android if it weren't for you.'

'So, why does it have to be my fault? Do you think I enjoyed finding out what I was?'

'Why should I have any opinions? I'm only an android.'

'All right,' sighed Gabrielle. 'I know you saved my life, but

135

when you have so much power why did you want to become like a human anyway?'

'I like the way it feels. It's comfortable and secure to have sensations flowing through you. You've always had them so you take them for granted.'

'You've only come across the better ones so far,' Gabrielle warned him. 'There are quite a few you might regret having. Have you felt fear, pain or anger yet?'

'I've got an idea I'm about to get the hang of those quite soon.'

'What do you mean?'

Weatherby laid his trenchcoat on the stone floor and invited her to sit beside him. When he was sure her anger was subsiding, he explained.

'I should have dismantled myself after you rectified the energy loss, but I didn't like the idea. The planet which was responsible for transmitting me tell me they have to keep to certain rules about androids and what they do on other planets and I am apparently breaking them. They have activated some service robots they keep at the bottom of the oceans here to come after me.'

'What will they do?'

'I'd rather not go into that. I've only got a rough idea and they're keeping the details as a surprise. But I know the robots are already here. I went to a bungalow at Heron's Point yesterday and it looked as though one of them had walked right through it. As soon as they get their eyesight and signal fixed they will be able to pull me to them like Wendle was pulled to that house . . . so I won't be bothering you or Penny much longer.'

'What will you tell Penny?' asked Gabrielle. 'You can't leave her thinking you might come back some day.'

'I'll think of something. I've still got some time before the power units I carry are absorbed.'

Knowing Weatherby was an android, Gabrielle was not able to comprehend the mixed emotions going through him. Absently, she lifted her hand to feel his hair and smooth skin.

'How on earth could all this be so realistic — And why choose that body? It was bound to attract attention.'

'So what's wrong with attracting attention? The other camouflage options were pretty insipid.'

'Oh . . . vanity.' A thought suddenly occurred to Gabrielle. 'You can't have children, can you?'

'No. That's one thing omitted from all android designs. I've only got the equipment, not the fuel.'

'If you think you are capable of becoming human, why shouldn't you be allowed to breed?' was Gabrielle's trick question.

'I don't know,' Weatherby had to confess.

'It's because you aren't really capable of developing a body like ours, isn't it? Let alone a spirit.'

Weatherby said nothing. Until it actually happened he could not be sure his anatomy would mature in the way it had been designed to.

'Give me a few more days,' he asked.

'What could I do about it anyway? Tell Penny you're an android from another planet sent to blow me up for stealing energy from the other side of the galaxy? She nearly fell over when I told her about Wendle being killed.'

'Once my power units are gone. I can't do anything about the robots. Then I'll be gone forever, I promise.'

'Why don't you just dismantle yourself, then?' Gabrielle suggested, not knowing how sick he was getting of the question.

'Why do you have to be so tough?' Weatherby asked.

'Perhaps it has something to do with survival?'

'So there's your answer.'

'Oh, all right,' Gabrielle eventually sighed. 'I won't tell Penny any dreadful stories to put her off you. Even young Paula's taken a fancy to you for some reason, and I don't want to be the one to shatter their illusions.'

'Thanks. I'll keep to my side of the bargain, I promise. I suppose I should be grateful I'm soon going to have the cure for my bad dreams.'

'You dream?'

'Sure,' replied Weatherby. 'Just as I was beginning to get some interesting ones about Penny, infernal creatures with big feet and decomposing complexions started trampling through them. You can't tell me you haven't had any bad dreams lately?'

'No. They stopped when I discovered what was happening.'

'You sound guilty about something.'

'Do I?' Gabrielle smiled, then said firmly, 'Let me know when your power units run down.' And before he could reply she left, wearing a secretive smile which added to his unease.

Paula and one of her friends were having a water battle over Weatherby's car in front of Penny's cottage later that day, instead of cleaning it in a more orthodox manner, while Penny and Weatherby sat in the cool of the living room talking about anything and everything but the way they felt about each other. Penny was not in a hurry to rush Weatherby to the registrar, then discover he had some mental imbalance like her first husband. The phone call she had received from Frank that morning was still fresh in her mind. This time he had delivered his threats so calmly and reasonably she had felt she had to phone Weatherby at his flat between shifts.

'We could have him picked up and warned,' Weatherby suggested, but Penny knew better.

'That would only make him worse. He's already got a persecution complex.'

'Perhaps if we were not to see each other for a little while?' Weatherby proposed carefully.

'Oh no. While I've got time off and you're not that busy it would be foolish.' She added carefully, 'You don't want to stop seeing me do you?'

'God, no,' Weatherby assured her before he thought of using the opportunity to keep his side of the bargain with Gabrielle. 'I never want to stop seeing you . . . but . . .'

'But what, Weatherby?'

'I may have to go away soon. I don't know when. I'll tell

you as soon as I do.'

Penny's spirits were dampened by the news. She fidgeted with the knitting on her lap, then suddenly announced, 'I think I'll just make a cup of tea.' She put her knitting aside and walked into the kitchen. 'I'm making a cup of tea!' Weatherby could hear her call into the front garden through the open door. 'Do you and Angela want one?'

'Yes please,' Paula's high-pitched voice screeched back. The chattering girl dashed into the room to give Weatherby a quick hug before joining Penny in the kitchen. He could feel everything he was learning to appreciate becoming a pleasant dream he would soon be woken from. Perhaps these were the sorts of dreams androids had, and reality was a matter manipulated by someone else.

20

Despite his better sense telling him to stay well clear of the coast, Weatherby was being driven out to the next sighting of slimy creatures from the deep by his enthusiastic young policewoman colleague. He had begun to have the uneasy feeling that Perkins trusted him to clear up the mystery within a few days. Having a fan as well as a lover did nothing to ease his anxiety. He was beginning to value Gabrielle's cool disregard which helped him keep his sense of proportion.

The nearness of this sighting also did nothing to reassure him that the robots were on the wrong track. Although he knew their signal would eventually be tuned into any part of the island to track him down he still preferred to be on the other side of it.

'Are you all right, sir?' Weatherby could hear a small voice at his elbow asking, and looked down to see Perkins watching him with fascinated interest. 'We're there.'

'Oh yes,' he said. 'So we are.'

They stepped out on to the rock-strewn wasteland beyond Wrecker's Cove and stared about them in bewilderment.

'Where do we start looking, sir?' she asked.

'Well, the fishermen must have been in line with the cove, and they said the shapes were just beyond that.' Weatherby told her, pointing into the distance. 'We'll have to walk, there's no way for the car to get round that rubble.'

Perkins locked the car and followed Weatherby's stride as he bounced from one loose rock to another.

'Might have been easier to have left the car in the village and walked along the top, sir?' she commented after ricking her ankle for the second time.

'We don't want to attract the village's attention and start rumours about this,' lied Weatherby, who preferred to keep

the sea at a safe distance. 'There must be enough of them circulating as it is.'

'Yes, of course. But how are we going to tell which of these holes was made by whatever they saw?'

'They measure approximately . . .' Weatherby said, taking out his notebook, 'Three and a half feet in diameter and two and a half feet deep. I don't know what that is in metric.'

'Well, they probably weren't French anyway,' giggled Perkins and Weatherby momentarily wished she could meet one.

Managing to cope with the terrain by springing like a small antelope from one rock to another, despite the regulation skirt, Perkins went well ahead of the less enthusiastic Weatherby who yelled after her, 'Do you want to encourage these things or something?'

'Well, we don't know what they are, do we, sir?' was the breezy reply.

'They are very heavy, short-sighted, and would probably find a young pink WPC very tasty.' Weatherby was convinced she thought it was all a game he had invented for the quiet season.

'Something just moved over there, sir.'

'Probably rabbits.'

'They must have a tough time burrowing through this stuff.' She laughed and pranced on her way. It was not until they were well past the spot that the remark struck Weatherby as being quite a logical one for her. What topsoil there was on that area of rock was not deep enough for overweight worms let alone rabbits. Like the good detective he was, he made a mental note to make sure he gave the spot a wide berth on the way back.

'Found anything, Perkins?' he eventually called to the sickeningly keen constable, hoping her answer would be a negative one. He could tell it was not going to be his lucky day when she replied, 'Over there, sir, I'm sure something moved just below the surface.' She bounded after it, only needing a butterfly net to make the picture complete.

'Come back!' Weatherby yelled with as much force as his vocal chords would allow, but she was already jabbing at the spot in the rubble with one of her shoes.

'I think it's all right, sir,' she called as Weatherby tried to reach her over the unsafe ground that separated them. 'Some rocks here have just been loosened by something.'

'Look, Perkins, don't argue or say anything, just move carefully away from there and away from me.' She turned to look at him in amazement. 'Back off girl, back off!'

Before Perkins was able to make a move, though, the thing Weatherby feared most began to happen. Like a minor eruption the ground lifted and solid rock split like cracked toffee. Slivers of granite flew in every direction, showering Perkins as she stood rooted to the spot.

'Run girl, run!' shouted Weatherby but, before she could follow his orders, a long swinging tentacle threshed through the air and sent her spinning into the track of the monster's massive feet.

Unable to think of anything more effective than heaving a rock at the creature, Weatherby hastily selected the heaviest he could find and hurled it at the evil slit-eyed head. It did succeed in attracting its attention long enough for Perkins to find her presence of mind and her feet and she leaped out of its path. The next second she was calling into her radio for assistance, watching powerlessly as the mountain of slime and tentacles turned its none too delicate attention to Weatherby.

'Run sir!' she called out. 'It'll never catch you if you run!' But she was not aware of the signal holding Weatherby's mind like a magnet. When he lifted his hands to clutch his head she thought he had been injured and, in the fashion of the truly reckless, ran after the towering monster and kicked as hard as she could at whatever part presented itself. Then, above the noise of their struggle, Perkins heard voices coming up from the coast path. A small crowd of people was rushing to their assistance, but as Perkins turned back she saw another of the creatures standing directly behind her.

'Why don't you run?' she shouted at Weatherby in rage and fright.

The answer was obvious. One of the creature's tentacles had gripped him securely around the body, and he was having enough trouble staying conscious. All he wanted was for Perkins to get further away so he could use what was left of his power units. His wish was answered from a most unlikely source. The other creature swished its tentacles through the air, and in its haste to get to Weatherby spun Perkins well away from the mêlée. By this time she was very stunned and dizzy, and did not see Weatherby energise his power units, to send a juddering jolt through both of the creatures just as they thought they had him securely. He was lucky that time. There was still enough power left to make them release their hold. By the time the villagers had stumbled over the rough ground to him and Perkins, the two robots were lumbering off, to disappear into a tunnel well concealed in the rock. Nobody offered to follow them.

Now the cat was out of the bag. Every available able-bodied person had run up the cliff path when the coastguard, who had been watching everything through his binoculars, had raised the alarm. And it was only minutes later that it seemed as though half the county's police force had turned up as well.

Weatherby and Perkins were escorted away with the reverence good clues deserve, and treated for cuts, bruises and shock by the district nurse. Weatherby refused to go to hospital, so Perkins boldly followed suit.

'You're a stupid woman,' Weatherby told her when they no longer had an audience. 'Why didn't you run when I told you?'

'And you are a stupid man, sir,' she replied, without so much as a blush on her bruised face. 'Why didn't *you* run when I said?'

'I had something on my mind. What's your reason?'

'I was scared stiff. And from where I was it looked as though you were as well.'

Weatherby dipped his head in embarrassment and started to grin, then laugh, though he was not quite sure why.

'Well, now,' Helto observed with wry amusement as she watched the monitor transmitting the signal from the robots. 'That was a good way of not attracting too much attention.'

'We will catch it the next time,' Insac assured her coolly.

'The Watchers will learn about this before then. You cannot perform exercises like that on a backward planet and not expect to be noticed.'

'Now we have the signal right, it won't happen again.'

'You're enjoying this aren't you?'

'No, I'm not, but I'll take over when the time comes if you want.'

'No. I'll do it.' Insac looked at her quizzically.

'I think it's self-aware. Its responses indicate a degree of bio-reaction. You might injure it.'

'All right, but you'll be impossible to work with afterwards.'

'That I promise,' Helto warned, 'and I want clearance to transmit a computer signal to Opu.'

'Why?'

'Just to report on the situation.' Helto said. 'What else?'

'All right, I'll give you the transmitter key. She should share some of the unpleasantness as her planet created the situation.'

Three nights later, Weatherby steeled himself to visit Penny and tell her he would be going. He had deliberately stayed away for fear of laying his explanation open to prolonged scrutiny. It was evening, but still light. He wanted to be sure Paula was in bed and wouldn't be brought into the arena as well.

As though she had been waiting for him, Penny opened the door before he could knock. He would not accept her invitation to go into the living room but stood with her in the

hall just by the open door.

'I can't stop, Penny,' he smiled weakly. 'But I had to see you before . . .' He could not bring himself to say any more.

'You're going after those creatures again, aren't you?' she demanded with surprising hardness.

He nodded, not able to tell her it was they who were after him. 'They think the night air is more likely to bring them out.'

'Why didn't you tell me what happened the other day? Didn't you trust me to know?'

Weatherby was confused by her intolerant attitude and muttered, 'But I didn't want to worry you . . .'

'It would have worried me a lot less if you'd said something instead of me having to hear about it through the gossips in the village shops.'

'Don't be angry. I'm trying to make it easy as I can.'

'Easy!' Penny nearly shouted, trying to keep her voice down. 'You stand there trying to tell me you won't be coming back because you're going out to get killed by some filthy slimy monster and expect me to accept it as though it was some normal hazard of life? Not even the police can make demands like that! This is what you meant when you told me you'd have to go away the other day, isn't it? At least I should be glad you've actually decided to tell me the truth.'

'But I don't want to be killed by some filthy slimy monster,' Weatherby protested. 'You're jumping to conclusions, Penny.'

'But you're trying to tell me there's a fair chance of it happening, aren't you?' Penny told him. 'The army should be dealing with this! I suppose as these things took a fancy to you the first time, they reckon they might want to come back for a second helping?'

Weatherby was so choked he could not argue with her, and only just managed to say, 'Please Penny . . . I don't want leave you, but if I'm not back by tomorrow morning then you'll know I'm dead and won't have to go on thinking I'm alive somewhere and hoping I'll return. I wouldn't want you

to spend your life wondering where I was.' He found a smile and her attitude softened.

'I know Weatherby,' Penny sniffed. 'I'm being unreasonable. I know there's probably not that much chance of your being killed, but when I saw those army trucks down the road I knew something serious was going on. I don't want to lose you either, you see.' She hugged him. 'I'll be here in the morning. Let me know you're all right as soon as you can . . . won't you?'

'I promised to see Gabrielle before I left,' he whispered in her ear. 'I'll let you break my ribs tomorrow.'

'All right,' said Penny, quickly releasing him. She suddenly remembered something. 'I want you to drop this in to her if you would.' She picked up a library book from the hall table. 'Then I can stay in all day waiting for news instead of delivering it myself.'

'Silly woman,' said Weatherby, taking the book and kissing her lightly on the lips. 'Say goodnight to Paula for me.'

'Oh, she probably heard every word,' Penny told him, but before she had finished speaking, he had fled out of the open door to his car.

21

As Weatherby stepped from the car he looked up at the cliff towards the setting sun and saw Gabrielle's silhouette.

'Don't let that watching from the top of the cliff develop into a habit,' he called out cheerfully to her. 'You know what happened to poor Wendle.' Then, as she did not reply, 'I've got to act as bait for the army where the robots appeared on the cliff the other day.'

At that, Gabrielle came slowly down and looked straight at him with a hypnotic, demanding stare.

'Penny sent this over,' Weatherby said handing her the library book but, as she took it, her gaze remained fixed on him. 'The power units have been absorbed,' he added casually. Her expression never flickered.

'Tell me, Weatherby,' Gabrielle suddenly asked. 'Have you ever experienced the feeling of hate?'

Weatherby looked at her in surprise, and thought carefully. 'No . . . not yet, anyway.'

'You know what is going to happen to you, but still don't hate anyone for it?'

'I probably don't like Penny's first husband too much, but he's most likely crazy, so he doesn't count. Why?'

'I just wanted to be sure of something.'

'I sometimes don't think you're quite human either.'

'I sometimes get the same feeling.'

'I reckon all this turmoil over the last couple of weeks or so has had an effect on you.'

'Right again,' Gabrielle said. 'Thanks for bringing the book. Goodbye, Weatherby.' Without another word she went inside the bungalow, leaving him wondering about the virtues of being human after all.

All Weatherby needed on top of his encounters with Penny

and Gabrielle was an unfriendly Major Clarke Johnson standing at the control point on top of the cliffs giving his opinions to the Captain of the army unit. He could hear the swift intake of breath as he approached and sensed the particular dislike the man had for him. Perhaps that was the hatred Gabrielle wanted to know if he felt?

'Taking your time, aren't you, Weatherby?' he snapped.

Weatherby replied sweetly, 'I'm sure they're not going to run away as soon as they know I'm here. Nice clear night for a bloody battle,' he added, to make sure everyone knew his opinion of professional fighters.

'Yes, well . . .' commented the Captain. 'Let's hope it doesn't come to that. How much do you think one of these landed leviathans weighs?'

'Too much,' muttered Weatherby under his breath, then, when he saw the Captain waiting for a reply, 'Several tons, I should think.'

'Can't be more specific can you, sir? We may need to use heavy artillery. Whatever they are, I only hope they're not some protected species the conservationists are liable to have our guts over.'

'Oh, no whale could be as stroppy as this pair.'

'They must have been three and a half tons each at least,' a voice piped up from the milling blue uniforms. Perkins's bruised face appeared, smiling from the throng as though she were on some picnic.

'Thank you, Miss,' sighed the Captain, obviously thinking them both mad. 'We'd better set the artillery up over there!' He shouted to his sergeant and went off to supervise the operation.

'What are you doing here, Perkins?' asked Weatherby disapprovingly.

'Why not, sir? Everybody else is, whether they're on duty or not.'

'You don't imagine for one moment that you're going up on to those cliffs and acting as bait, do you?'

'Well of course, Isn't that what you're going to do?'

'Oh no you're not.'

'Why not, sir?

'Because it's obvious pink can't be their colour after all. They seem to have preferred the taste of an aging black detective. Now get back to the control unit before I handcuff you to a lamp-post.'

'Aren't any about here, sir.' Perkins, seeing a look of thunder pass over Weatherby's usually amiable features, backed away. 'All right, sir. If you insist.'

'You can look after this for me.' He took off his jacket and handed it to her. 'Just in case I have to run.'

'You will this time, then, sir?'

'Promise,' lied Weatherby with a smile, then waved her away.

Major Clarke Johnson had watched their little discussion with stern disapproval and Weatherby thought he would like to tell him what in fact was going to happen, just to see what his reaction would be, but thought better of it just in time. The Captain was calling to him from the higher ground where the gun was being erected and, beaming the Major a quick insincere smile, he made his way towards it.

'I think if you were to walk in a semicircle from the path on the cliff edge to see how our lights pick you out to begin with . . .' the Captain mused.

'Fine,' agreed Weatherby. 'But how well these creatures know it's a trial run?'

'Oh, don't go too far to begin with, and there's still some light. I'll be sending armed men with you when you go round the next time.' Then the Captain murmured to himself, 'Pity I can't catch one whole; give the men a challenge.' Aloud he said, 'Don't worry, sir, they are crack marksmen.'

'Thanks. I promise to look after them.'

'It was one of the conditions of letting you do this, Weatherby,' said a stern voice which was capable of striking genuine apprehension into his heart, and Weatherby turned to the shadows from whence it came and saw his Commissioner. 'As soon as these creatures arrive, you are to get out

of there and leave everything to the army. D'you understand?'

'Yes, sir,' Weatherby could almost feel his body standing to attention against his will.

'And don't go and fall down some pothole like a ruddy fool. Good luck.' Before Weatherby could reply, he was gone.

Weatherby began to marvel at the attention he was receiving prior to doing his brave deed, and wondered what splendid niceties would be lavished on his mortal remains — if they were ever found reasonably near each other. He tried to entertain himself with the thought that androids could not feel pain. When he was isolated in the limpid gleam of the searchlights though, and too far from the heavy artillery for comfort, he could feel his mortal knees take on the tension of jelly. In a cold sweat, he was relieved to get back to the footpath again and let the cool night breeze erase the tell-tale traces of perspiration from his body before he reached the Captain.

'Splendid, splendid,' the Captain said, after having had him lined up in the sights of the gun as well as the search lights. 'Nothing would stand a chance from here.'

'Including me,' Weatherby answered in his thoughts.

'We're ready to go now,' said the Captain, coughing abruptly to attract Weatherby's attention. 'You can make the circle a bit wider now. I'll have four men follow directly after you.'

'Right,' said Weatherby, and started out once more over the treacherous landscape.

As the reality of the situation slowly crept up on him, Weatherby began to wish there were no soldiers to see his apprehension. They were obviously not expecting some slimy monstrous thing to rise from the depths of solid rock to order as he was. Time passed, and Weatherby felt a little more reassured when not so much as a flaw appeared in the rocky ground. By the time they were on their third circuit, he was feeling bold enough to lead them even further out, and had to

be warned by the Corporal.

'Better keep in range of the gun, sir. We don't know how good these rifles would be if we meet one of these things,' he said in such a way as to suggest he was becoming bored with the whole business and the appearance of a monster would be a welcome relief.

Weatherby obeyed him, straightening his path towards the edge of the cliff, where they had not been before. The ground was a little easier, and he made his way unsuspectingly to the perimeter of the searchlights. That was his fatal mistake. Had the searchlight reached further it would probably have picked out the grotesque shape waiting in the mouth of a tunnel to make its clumsy pounce.

Weatherby had not felt any signal tugging at his brain, so let out a startled yelp of surprise when the robot's tentacles suddenly snaked round his body and grasped him tight. In the next instant the soldiers were in position, firing at the creature's head, while the heavy gun had to sit idly silent while Weatherby tried to struggle free. Then another searchlight picked out the robot's companion, lumbering towards the party. The gun crew trained their sights on it before it got too close to the other. With a loud report that shook the watching village a shell smashed into its target, but as the smoke cleared they could see that the creature had managed to quicken its pace, without even minor damage. The Captain went several shades of red, white and blue in rage, terror and shock, as he realised he was going to be the unfortunate to have to explain this in a report.

'Fire again before it gets any closer,' he ordered, with more than a tinge of desperation in his voice, and the blast drowned his next order to the assembled armed men to charge over the terrain.

He was too late. The monsters had escaped down a tunnel with Weatherby and sealed its entrance. By the time the smoke cleared and the soldiers had reached the spot where Weatherby had put up his struggle with the two robots, all trace of them was gone. The four soldiers were in a state of

shock, too blinded by smoke to tell which way they had gone. Some vainly tried to follow their elephantine tracks, but the ground was too pitted to sort them out in the dark. Even when the Commissioner made his thorough way over the scene of the crime, he could find nothing but the fob watch Weatherby had worn ever since his metal watch strap had burned an old man's hand.

'We'll have to start a search in the morning,' he was eventually resigned to admitting.

As the Commissioner flanked by several of his officers made his impressive way through the silent gathering in the village below, Dot whispered into Gabrielle's ear, 'Don't think we should say anything to your Aunt Penny about this, should we, dear?'

'From here we can't be too sure what happened,' Gabrielle replied. 'And they aren't likely to tell us, or the press.'

'No. But I can take a good guess.'

'Poor Weatherby.' Gabrielle smiled wryly. 'Penny will never get over this.'

'They took it to the nearest station,' Insac told Helto as she came back on shift and took her place before the monitor. 'I sent the robots back. I won't cocoon them until we've finished, though. The tunnels will have to be serviced.'

'I suppose they succeeded in totally disrupting the life of the area before they went?' Helto thought there was something wrong with Laws that allowed lumbering great monsters like that on other peoples' planets, but not seemingly inoffensive androids.

'Now we have it, don't take too long in carrying out the scan. Send the results to the engineers as soon as you have them. Make sure they are thorough. We may not get another chance to find out why this particular type of machine malfunctions.' A thought struck Insac as he was about to leave. 'Are you sure you want to do this?'

'I'll do it. You know you can trust me.'

'Yes, I know I can.' Insac left her to get on with the job.

Helto turned her attention to the monitor as soon as he had gone. She could see Weatherby's body clearly, pinned flat between two pillows of air pressure, strong enough to prevent him from moving, but not to prevent the laboratory equipment from operating about him.

'Hello, Kybion infant.' Helto said to the monitor, 'Why did you have to be so foolish?'

Weatherby was unable to answer the voice coming from the ceiling which he was compelled to stare at, because there was a tube in his mouth flushing fluid through his digestive tract. Though not painful, this was undignified, and also he did not welcome a one-sided conversation with the ceiling.

'I'm sorry if you find this unpleasant,' Helto said. 'But everything must be thoroughly clean before we can place the

scanning equipment inside you. You would insist on developing the sort of biology we can't take apart and test. The service robots have gone now. There's no need to worry about them.'

Weatherby pondered whether it would have been better for him if they had managed to tear him apart, as he unsuccessfully tried to flex his muscles to ease the discomfort of the pump.

'Don't try to struggle. Nothing I do will hurt you.' As though she could hear Weatherby mentally calling her a liar, she added, 'Well, I will make everything as easy as possible.'

There was something calm and slow in her tones that suggested she was going to take as long as she possibly could and Weatherby wondered whether she was going to let his newly acquired bowels be washed away completely.

'I will remove the pump soon,' she promised.

He felt a spray of fluid saturate his body. This was a welcome relief from the pummelling going on inside him. Then Helto removed the pump.

'Thanks . . .' Weatherby managed to gasp in relief. 'Why couldn't you just have me put down first, then go through all this?'

'Of course we couldn't. What would we be able to tell from your body reactions if they were no longer functioning?'

'That I was dead.'

'You are very sensitive for an android.'

'Those who designed me will no doubt be very pleased to know that. But it doesn't do me much good here and now.'

'If you weren't tense, none of this would hurt so much. Why not try to relax?'

'Because I'm scared bloody stiff of what you're going to think up next,' Weatherby admitted. 'Can't you understand that I'm not one of your mindless mechanical mistakes? I'm delicate and don't like being patronised.'

Helto pondered for a moment. 'You do sound very much like a human. I would like to run a scan to see whether your

voice pattern matches. It will be some while before we have the other results.'

'I don't need to be told whether I'm real or not. I can feel it.'

'Interesting . . .' Helto saw all the more reason for her delaying tactics.

Sterilising jets cleansed every part of Weatherby's body and, after a while, he found it quite relaxing, but this made him wonder all the more about the inspection probe which would be placed inside him.

'How are you going to insert the scanning equipment?' he eventually found the courage to ask.

'Oh, we aren't going to cut you up,' Helto reassured him, but refrained from answering the question.

When Gabrielle returned to the silence of the bungalow, she made herself a cup of coffee and took it to the settee where she sat with her legs tucked beneath her, thinking. She carefully watched the time on the well-polished face of the old grandfather clock, apparently the only furniture from his own time that Wendle had possessed. As the brass hands drew near midnight she let her legs relax into a more comfortable position and closed her eyes to drop into a controlled doze.

Slowly her conscious thoughts moved out of her sleeping body. The next instant she was standing in the laboratory deep in the Earth's crust where Weatherby was being held captive, and then she stood at the shoulder of Helto herself as she talked to him from her monitor and tapped the console in irritation, casting anxious glances at a row of unlit signal lights.

'You will not feel anything,' she was telling Weatherby on the monitor as one of the laboratory machines fed a fine transparent cord into his mouth. This was pulled down into his body by drawing a beam over his stomach.

To Weatherby's surprise and relief she was right. Helto

altered the air pressure surrounding him so his body could rest in a more natural position.

'I'll do the brain scan now, then you can rest.'

By the way Helto was playing for time, Gabrielle knew she must act quickly. Now in total command of her Star Dancer nature, she selected the route to Ojal. She could let it dawdle and gawp at the wonders of the universe another time.

An unsuspecting Anaru sat cross-legged about to activate the loop. As soon as she had the ability to see and hear her, Gabrielle demanded, 'Fetch Controller Opu.'

Anaru looked straight into the demanding dark eyes of a very serious human being. She almost leaped out of the loop in surprise, but had the presence of mind not to shut the power down before dashing to her alcove to send out the call.

Opu was not in the control room or her own home, and it was only by pure chance that Anaru found her about to leave Annac's home with her small brat. Noting the urgency in Anaru's garbled message, Opu gave Annac the dubious pleasure of looking after Opuna while she flew off to find out what the trouble was.

When Opu arrived and joined the loop, she was as amazed as Anaru to see the Star Dancer.

'I am able to talk to you now,' Gabrielle told them without waiting to formally introduce herself.

'What do you want?' Opu asked, still fearful of the power she knew the creature must possess.

'You received a message from Taigal Rax informing you about the android you designed together to send to Earth?'

'You mean Perimeter 84926? Yes. It was malfunctioning, so they are going to dismantle it. What's wrong in that?'

'Have you tried to prevent this?'

'Of course not. Apart from not wanting to interfere after they had helped us, it would have been against the Law to let it wander about on that planet. We don't want any trouble. We've had all we need for a long while.'

'You must contact Taigal Rax and tell them to stop this.'

'But I can't,' protested Opu. 'I don't like the idea of having

to break up something as sophisticated as that, but there's no way we can get it back.'

'You must leave it where it is.'

'But that would bring the collected wrath of the Watchers down on us, human. Don't you understand the price of evolution is self-control?'

'The Law must have already been broken by the robots sent after it. Send the signal now, before it is too late.'

'Why all this over one android?'

'Although there may not be much time,' Gabrielle said, 'I will tell you why.'

Weatherby felt surprisingly refreshed after the short rest Helto had allowed him following the brain scan. There had been nothing unpleasant about that either, though the barrage of sound waves did make his skull vibrate a little. The more relaxed position he had been moved into helped to ease his dismayed digestive tract, and he even found himself becoming interested in what Helto was doing.

'Why are you taking so long over this?' he asked when she had finished transmitting the information about his brain to those who had helped design it.

'Would you rather I rushed things?' Helto inquired, hoping he was not in too much of a hurry to be dismantled.

'No. As long as you keep it painless I'm happy to go on living for as long as you like.' He could hear a voice in the background asking Helto, 'Is that all you've done?'

'That's right. You said everything would have to be thorough.'

'Well, it doesn't make any difference to me,' Insac's voice echoed clearly from the ceiling. 'It will make a lot of difference to the android though if it's as sophisticated as those brain scans show. Do you want me to take over?'

'No, no,' Weatherby could hear Helto's voice faintly scolding. 'Just go away.'

Weatherby was not sure whether to panic right away, or

wait until he found out what was going to happen. The fact that Helto did not speak to him for a painful length of time did not help to reasssure him.

'We have to go on to the body scan now,' her voice suddenly announced.

Weatherby had quite forgotten the cord threaded into his body and wondered how that could have been the cause of the exchange between Helto and her unknown companion.

'What happens?' he asked, half preferring the opportunity of dying of surprise when he found out.

'Don't you trust me?' Helto asked carefully.

'If you are going to have to dismantle me at any moment that seems somewhat irrelevant.'

'I meant, could you believe I might be trying to help you?'

'No,' said Weatherby. 'Why should I?'

' I cannot tell you.' No sooner had she uttered those words than Weatherby felt an odd crawling sensation in his stomach, as though something was moving about inside him.

When he was sure it was not butterflies, he demanded, 'What is that?'

'The body scan. It shouldn't be painful.'

As the crawling sensation began to spread, and he felt as though every organ in his body was being poked and squeezed, he blurted out, 'I prefer pain.'

'It's only caused by the impulses planted around your organs by the scan cord.'

'I don't care,' called Weatherby through gritted teeth, 'I don't like it.' Then, as the bruising sensations intensified, 'Can't you turn it off?'

'Don't panic. When it's finished the cord will dissolve.'

That information was lost on Weatherby as he looked down at his body and saw the scanning impulses glowing through his skin.

Helto had to switch off the receiver in the room so the sounds of his protests did not distract her from collating the incoming information. She shot an occasional glance towards the line of signal lights, but nothing there interrrupted her

gathering and transmitting of information. Helto wished she had the callousness to prolong the body scan but, realising from the results that he was no longer an android, she weakened and slowly let the scan run down. Then she reopened the receiver and sat looking blankly at the semi-conscious Weatherby.

Insac returned, and saw Helto sitting by the completed information, looking vacantly at the monitor. Seeing the state Weatherby was in, he told her, 'You've got to finish now. It's pointless leaving it in that condition.'

'I know.' She sighed in resignation and, with one last look towards the signal lights, Helto pushed the control which operated the beam that would dismember his body.

'I can't stand this . . .' Insac muttered to himself as the reality of what they were doing dawned on him.

'It's probably better to do it before he recovers,' Helto said. 'Do you still feel like taking over?'

'No thanks, I'm beginning to feel a bit strange about it myself.'

'What for? This is our job. To maintain and control robots and androids we have planted on other planets, and break them up when they don't do as they are told.'

'Look through these results,' Insac said. 'They actually did it. They made an android that could turn into a living being. There was nothing wrong with it after all.'

'Well, let's hope there's a law passed soon so we don't have to go through all this again.' Helto activated the beam. 'I'll remove the head first. It's the best way.'

Constable Perkins spent all night trying to keep out of everyone's way as she carried on her own search for her detective companion. She had been ordered off duty for rest and recuperation after the battering she had received from the marauding monsters, but nobody had noticed her presence in the confusion of the night before. The only thing she managed to find out, however, was that Gabrielle was a close friend of his, and where she lived.

About six o'clock in the morning there were only three policemen patrolling the beach and village, waiting for the search party to arrive. Perkins was exhausted by that time, and wanted to rest, but couldn't bring herself to go home while her superior was still missing. Then she remembered Gabrielle. She easily found her bungalow and gingerly knocked on the door. To her amazement it was immediately opened by a fully-dressed girl who looked as though she had been wide awake for hours.

'I hope you don't mind me calling on you at this time in the morning?' Perkins began, but Gabrielle waved her inside. 'I'm Perkins,' she added.

'I can tell,' said Gabrielle with a smile. 'Weatherby's told me about you. You look as though you've been up all night.'

'I've been looking for Mr Weatherby, but I daren't be seen by one of the others or they'll only order me to go home.'

'Well — if you will go about attacking slimy monsters from the deep!' Gabrielle poured her a cup of tea. 'Why not drink this and get a couple of hours sleep?'

'I don't think I could. I can't stop thinking about what happened to Mr Weatherby.'

'Oh he's all right. He's grown his own self-preservation

unit.' This only helped to reduce Perkins to tears.

'He was such a lovely man,' she blubbered until Gabrielle handed her a tissue. 'You should have seen what happened to him up there . . . it was terrible.'

'Look, why don't you have a short sleep, then we'll go and search along the beach together?'

'All right,' Perkins agreed.

'I'll wake you up in a couple of hours,' Gabrielle promised. 'You'll feel a lot better then.'

Controller Opu dashed through the air like a thing possessed as she headed towards her control. Other Ojalies had learned to get out of her flight path by now, and she fell to the floor of the balcony without having caused any major mid-air disasters on the way. 'If Annac hadn't taken away the link Anaru had with Taigal Rax there would be no need for this,' she told herself as she pounced on the console, much to the surprise of the controller operating it.

As she tried to switch into the computer transmission, the controller asked her, 'Didn't you know the computer link was severed shortly after that transmission from Taigal Rax? Something to do with gravitational interference.' Opu did not say a word, but swayed gently before making a dash to the balcony where she sprinted into the air again, only bothering to open her wings after she was airborne.

'What was all that about?' asked the startled controller.

'No idea,' mused another. 'But you know what she can get like. After the emergency and having to look after that brat of hers, it isn't surprising.'

Annac, whose curiosity had got the better of her, had just arrived at Anaru's house and made Opuna secure in her light cubicle. She was in time to see Opu pile up on the small balcony behind the light beam curtain.

'The link's been severed,' Opu gasped. 'Interference of some sort. Get Healphani on the loop quick.'

'But I can't do that,' Anaru protested. 'It's nothing like the correct transmission time.'

'If we can't get a message through stopping them from dismembering that andriod, we'll have more trouble than a dozen Star Dancers.'

'Why?' said Annac, had no idea what was going on.

'I don't have time to tell you. Please try, Anaru. You heard what was said, and know what is going to happen if we can't reach them.'

'From the way Healphani spoke, it seems as though it must already be too late.' Anaru could see Opu was not going to be fobbed off so easily. 'Oh, all right, then, but I'm afraid that android will be spare parts by the time I make contact.' She switched on the power.

'Android?' queried Annac. 'Why all this bother about an android?'

'Because it isn't an android any more,' Opu told her.

'You mean the one you used the Kybini System to transmit to Perimeter 84926 actually developed into a living thing?' she chortled in delight. 'That's marvellous.'

'It's not if you're the android at the moment, or us if we can't stop it from being broken up.'

'But what's the problem? You sound as though the Star Dancer is threatening to come back?' Opu was suspiciously quiet, so Annac went on, 'If it was an android once, then it can't be registered as anything else.'

'There is no known precedent,' Opu told her. 'Androids can be dismantled, but living creatures can't.'

'Ah . . .' a glimmer of understanding showed on Annac's face. 'I knew those robot engineers would get too clever for their own good one day.'

'Shut up, you two, I'm trying to concentrate,' Anaru said, as she transmitted her thoughts at Taigal Rax with every ounce of will she had. After a while she said, 'It's no good. They're just not expecting us at the moment.'

'Try scanning the planet,' Opu told her. 'Get hold of anyone you can.'

'But only someone like Healphani would be believed carrying a message like that.'

'I'll give the code to the first person you contact,' Opu promised. Annac and Anaru stared at her in amazement. 'It's the only way.'

'You mean it was *her*?' gasped Annac in alarm, and even Opu's child stopped trying to escape from the light cubicle on the other side of the room and intently watched what was going on. 'That could be pretty serious.'

'Well, I wouldn't like to fail in getting this message through just to find out what happens,' Opu told her.

'And I always thought that android was so incompetent.'

'It wasn't, apparently. It was too efficient.'

They sat watching Anaru's screen in silence. Nothing happened for a painfully long while, and Annac whispered to Opu, 'But surely she could have gone straight to Taigal Rax?'

'It would have taken her too long to make contact there. At least we recognised her.'

'It's not much quicker this way . . .'.

Something shuddered on to the screen. 'What is that?' Annac asked in amazement as she joined the loop.

A wide-skulled, black-scaled creature peered back in amazement at them. It blinked in disbelief once or twice, then some of its babbling thoughts spluttered into the loop.

'I knew I should stop trying to dive to these depths. I'm beginning to hallucinate now.'

'Can you see us?' Anaru demanded with such authority the diver replied despite himself. 'I can see something, and I can hear something inside my skull as well.'

'That's me talking to you. There is nothing wrong with you. You are not hallucinating. You are a sensitive.'

'Who, me?' inquired the diver incredulously. 'I'm only a maintenance diver. And I'm only that because I'm not bright enough to be anything else. Me a sensitive? Never.'

'If that's all the use you are then,' interrupted Opu, 'It won't be beneath you to deliver a message for us to your nearest control station.'

163

'You're not playing a trick on me, are you?' the black-scaled diver inquired suspiciously.

'What do we have to say to convince you that you are a sensitive who has it in his power to save someone's life?'

'Oh . . . I suppose that's different then. What do you want me to do?'

'You must remember a code symbol, and a simple message. You have to concentrate very deeply while we put the symbol into your mind.'

'Oh, I'm no good at remembering things.'

'You must try.'

'But I'm so useless at remembering things I have to carry an instruction board with me all the time or I forget what I'm supposed to be doing,' the diver explained. 'I daren't go anywhere without it.'

'Well, draw it on that while we put it in your mind,' Opu ordered him in a near frenzy, so Anaru had to remind her, 'Keep calm, keep calm. You can't rush this fellow.'

'All right,' the diver said as he lifted his board and held a writing instrument over it in readiness. Anaru and Opu jointly drew the symbol in their minds and the diver laboriously copied it on to the board. They could see it adequately resembled what they had transmitted, then Opu carefully told him, 'Now write this beneath it. Ready?'

'Ready.'

'The Kybion . . . not . . . to . . . be . . . dismantled . . . Opu.'

Not knowing he was being transmitted the words by somebody with a completely alien tongue, the diver automatically wrote it down in his own language; Opu could not know if he had it right or wrong.

'Is that all?' the bewildered diver asked.

'It is. Remember, if you do not hurry to the nearest station and hand that message over, someone will die.'

'All right,' the diver assured them, obviously deciding to believe the conversation that had gone on in his head had been real. He turned to swim off in such a leisurely way that

the other three wondered whether his good intentions were going to be enough.

'He'll never make it in time wherever the nearest station is,' sighed Opu and buried her beak in her hands.

'Oh, don't worry too much,' Annac told her. 'By the shape of his body and colouring he must have been at quite a depth and won't be able to move faster until he reaches the surface.'

'I hope you're right . . . I just hope you're right.' Opu turned in time to see her brat scrambling out of the light cubicle and advancing towards her. 'Now what do you want?' she asked irritably. In reply her child sank its beak into her arm in an affectionate bite. 'I suppose that serves me right for asking,' Opu rubbed the wound. 'I'm sure after all our evolution she's a throwback.'

Weatherby's body throbbed so much after the scanning device had finished with it he did not even try to struggle as he saw the beam hover menacingly over his head. Instead, as it snaked down towards him, he closed his eyes tight and hoped it would be quick. All the while he could hear Insac's and Helto's voices above.

'Use more power,' Insac was saying. 'It'll make a cleaner incision.'

Weatherby could feel the heat of the beam as Helto did as he said.

'He's so tense it'll be impossible to be very accurate,' Helto complained. 'Are you sure there isn't any way to stun him?'

'Not effectively. Androids have never needed anaesthetics before.'

Now Weatherby felt the beam lined up with his neck and tried to faint, but he was too aware of his aching insides. He heard Helto calling, 'Quick, answer that.'

'All right,' Insac replied. Then, after a brief pause, 'Cut that thing out quick.'

He was obviously not referring to Weatherby's neck as the

beam promptly disappeared. His arms were suddenly free of the pressure on them and he was able to flex his muscles for the first time in hours. Still the conversation above went on.

'This is from Opu,' Insac announced.

'Yes,' said Helto. 'I did contact her, remember.'

'But what about this code? Who else did you contact when I gave you the transmitter key?' There was a pause as Insac checked the console. 'There's been interdimensional traffic on here quite recently.'

'Yes . . .' mused Helto. 'Isn't technology wonderful?'

The last few words were lost on Weatherby, who slid into a deep sleep.

24

After some time standing on top of the cliff, scouring every inch of sea and beach lit by the early morning sun, Gabrielle saw what she was looking for and went back to the bungalow to rouse Perkins. Still only half awake, and without waiting to put on her tie, jacket or hat, or bothering to tuck her shirt into her skirt, Perkins followed Gabrielle outside.

As they approached the shore down a twisting path Gabrielle pointed out a crumpled heap lying at the water's edge. Although her guide seemed to know what it was, Perkins was unable to fathom its relevance as the sun's rays glistened on the wet bundle.

The nearer they got, the more familiar the clothes it wore became. The waistcoat was unmistakable. With a bound of joy Perkins ran past Gabrielle's measured stride, calling out to the soaked body, 'Mr Weatherby, Mr Weatherby, are you all right?'

She hauled him into a sitting position, without first bothering to find out whether he was conscious.

Weatherby's eyes suddenly opened wide in amazement as he saw Perkins kneeling beside him and felt her fingers sink into his tender flesh.

'Say something, sir. Say something,' she was demanding.

'Perkins . . .' He winced at her none too delicate attention. 'You are improperly dressed.'

Perkins saw nothing unusual in this remark and took it to mean he was feeling as well as could be expected.

'Haven't you anything else to say to us?' Gabrielle inquired as she approached them. Weatherby thought in wide-eyed confusion for a moment, unable to work out how he had got there and why his body throbbed so much that even the pressure of his buttoned waistcoat was distressing.

'I can't think of anything. Only, undo my waistcoat one of you — carefully!' he added as Perkins immediately obliged with her usual enthusiasm.

'There's something wrong with his body,' Gabrielle told Perkins. 'We'll have to try and walk him to the bungalow. Be careful to only take his arms to support him.'

Somehow they managed to struggle to the top of the cliff with him and there Weatherby shook them off. Perkins wanted to call for an ambulance, but he was adamant she should not. and refused even to let her tell anyone else he had been found. Perkins was mystified by his sudden attack of aloofness and insistence on making the rest of his way to the bungalow unaided. He pushed even Gabrielle away as though she had the evil eye.

'Now we have to inform the others out there searching for you,' Gabrielle told Weatherby in a no-nonsense way when they reached the living room. 'Perkins has the keys to your car and flat and she can do that when she goes to fetch a change of clothes for you.'

He allowed them to ease him on to the settee, where he sat looking too tired and haggard to argue.

'You'll have to have a doctor as well.'

'No!' Weatherby insisted weakly. 'I don't want any doctor near me.'

'He's just being irrational,' Gabrielle told Perkins. 'Do you feel up to doing all that?'

'Oh yes,' she agreed brightly, obviously her old scatter-brained self again at finding her lost head boy, even though whatever he had been through had not improved his manners.

She hastily pulled on the rest of her uniform and sped out of the door as though promotion depended on it.

'I don't want to see anyone,' Weatherby complained.

'I know,' sympathised Gabrielle, 'But the effects won't last forever.'

Weatherby looked up at her uncertainly, 'Do you know what happened?'

'Yes.'

'Then it must have been you who stopped them.'

'I did have something to do with it.'

'You threatened Ojal with the Star Dancer again, didn't you? You'll let all hell loose if you've done that. You will have committed a crime in the eyes of Galactic Law!'

'Don't fret so. Nothing dreadful is going to happen.'

'But you don't know what you've done. It would have been better to have left me.'

'It's all right,' she told him, gently patting his head and neck dry with a towel. 'I'll explain it all to you as a wedding present.'

'I thought you were glad to see me go.' Weatherby said in annoyance and confusion.

'Now, don't get angry. Perhaps I've grown fond of you as well in a funny sort of way.'

'I wouldn't have guessed.'

'At one time you had access to more knowledge than every library and computer bank on this planet and all you could use it for was to become romantic. A creature like you deserves to be understood by someone else.'

'So what happens now?' Weatherby asked, thinking of the Watcher that was bound to catch up with them sooner or later.

'Nothing,' Gabrielle insisted. 'You're quite safe.'

'But after what you've done? You just don't understand, do you?'

'Believe me, Weatherby, there is nothing to fret about from now on. The only planet that need concern you is this one.' He wanted to believe her and tears of anger began to fill his eyes because he could not. 'And don't start snivelling. Half the county's police force and umpteen soldiers will probably turn up on the doorstep any minute.'

'You're mad,' he sniffed, deciding to enjoy what time he had left, as though the inevitable retribution of the Watchers would be nothing more than another unlikely dream.

It did not take long for Gabrielle to find a dressing-gown of

Wendle's for Weatherby to slip on after she had helped remove his wet clothes. Though Wendle had been much smaller, it did manage to cover his body without discomfort or embarrassment until his own clothes turned up via a breathless Perkins.

When the police arrived Weatherby was unable to think of any story more plausible than what had actually happened to him. He told them he must have lost consciousness when the creatures carried him off, and stayed that way until he woke up on the beach. Medical examination confirmed the presence of internal bruising which had been caused by the sort of pressure the creatures could have inflicted when they seized him, and everyone seemed happy enough to accept those explanations.

Weatherby received a medal far more splendid than the one he had previously hoped for from his Commissioner.

When the news leaked out, the village suffered the occasional influx of psychics and UFO spotters, but the district never increased its number of holidaymakers. For some reason most people were not anxious to meet slimy, lumbering monsters and shake one of their many tentacles, even though the creatures did not come back.

Apart from the brief phone call Gabrielle made that morning from the sea-front telephone kiosk to tell her that Weatherby was safe, Penny knew nothing of what had gone on. This did not bother her too much because she was very good at guessing. She had not left the cottage in case Weatherby arrived or phoned. Knowing he was safe, she cursed herself for being so hysterical about his going in the first place. All she wanted to do when she saw him standing at the front door in his shirtsleeves was to deliver the long hard hug she had started to give him the night before. It must have been extremely uncomfortable for Weatherby, but he said nothing until Penny noticed the inflamed condition of his body through the thinness of his shirt.

'Why aren't you wearing your waistcoat, Weatherby?' she

asked, suddenly releasing him. 'I've never known you without it before?'

'I must be putting on weight,' he lied. 'I had trouble doing the buttons up. Why, do you only want to hug me when I've got a waistcoat on?' He tried to embrace her, but she backed away, fixing him with a suspicious look.

'Come inside, Weatherby,' Penny said calculatingly.

Weatherby did as he was told, getting used to her sudden changes of mood. She herded him into the living room and closed the door behind her.

'Now what?' asked Weatherby, not sure what to make of it all.

'Take your shirt off,' she commanded.

'Why?' he laughed, but Penny was not put off.

'We aren't teenage sweethearts, Weatherby. We're adults. And if neither of us can trust the other to tell them things that matter, we might as well be strangers.'

Weatherby was unsure what to do. He tugged half-heartedly at his tie and kept throwing sidelong glances in Penny's direction to see if there was any chance of her changing her mind.

Penny saw his reluctance. 'I don't mind you not wanting to talk about your past life or how many lovers you've had. I know you'd never be a policeman if you had a record or were mentally disturbed. And I don't particularly want to talk about my past, but I do mind you keeping things from me that matter now. I want to know when there's a chance of you being killed or injured . . . And I want to know when you *have* been injured. It's all right, Paula's playing round at her friend's, so don't worry about her bursting in.'

Weatherby still hesitated. 'Do you want us to get married?' she asked. He looked up as though wondering how she could have doubted it. 'Then take that shirt off now,' she insisted. 'I have a right to know what's underneath it.'

With no way of avoiding it, Weatherby slowly undid his shirt and removed it.

'How did it happen?' Penny demanded when she saw his

swollen body, but the tears Gabrielle had made him suppress welled up and he was unable to say anything. 'Why aren't you in hospital?' she chided.

'I wouldn't like the food,' he choked. 'And I wouldn't want to make you travel all that way every time you wanted to scold me.'

'Oh, Weatherby. I wouldn't scold you if you trusted me.' She kissed him as passionately as his delicate condition would allow.

'When?' asked Weatherby eventually.

'When what?'

'When are we going to be married? You are sure you want marry me, aren't you, Penny?'

'Looks as though I'll have to now I've made you take your shirt off. Let's wait until my brother and his wife can get down here, then they can stop with Gabrielle.'

'Paula won't mind us getting married?' Weatherby asked unsurely.

'I'm sure she won't. When we have our honeymoon she can stop with Gabrielle as well.'

'Gabrielle might not appreciate all that company,' Weatherby warned her.

'Of course she won't mind for a couple of weeks. I don't know why you two are so funny about each other.'

'We're probably kindred spirits in a way.'

'How do you mean?' asked Penny.

'Oh . . . she knows what she wants, but won't tell anyone else what it is. I know what I want and everyone in the universe knows I've got it.'

Penny laughed at what she took to be a flight of fancy and kissed him again.

Later that summer Gabrielle, still living in the bungalow Wendle had left her, began working part time in the village library. Her foster parents, Jack and Connie, had arrived a week before to attend the wedding to be held in the town's registry office. They spent most of their time making plans for the reception to follow in the village hotel.

Weatherby had made a habit of turning up at Penny's every evening, or sending Perkins over to make sure she had not run off with someone else. Even Perkins began to believe she would be glad when her superior was safely married. The only one getting the best out of the situation was Paula, who relished the prospect of being bridesmaid at her mother's wedding.

There was very little formality in the service at the registry office. All concerned, especially Weatherby, were too anxious to get it over with. The main point of interest with the guests was where Weatherby had managed to find the astonishing waistcoat that clashed so well with Penny's brocade two-piece.

After the dash to the hotel reception, and obligatory speeches, few people seemed to notice that the couple they had been toasting were nowhere to be found. Not seeing why a mature couple should have exercised any more self-control than younger ones, nobody tried to look for them. No one except a striking-looking girl with the penetrating gaze of a mystic. Weatherby and Penny knew Gabrielle was only a short distance away from them in the hotel garden. From where she was she seemed to be watching everything but what they were doing.

Gabrielle had become much more mature, and mysterious, in a very short while. Connie and Jack were delighted with

the change, and pleased she was so independent, and growing into a woman without any of the traumas of the young. Only to Weatherby had her development appeared to be inexplicably sinister. This caused him to be apprehensive for reasons it was impossible for him to share. He always had at the back of his mind the terror of Penny finding out the truth about him and the pending retribution of the Watchers on Gabrielle and himself. It would have eased his mind a little if the girl had been at least half as concerned as he was, but he fancied some sort of madness was preventing her from realising the gravity of their situation.

'What are you thinking about?' smiled Penny at Weatherby's sudden thoughtfulness. The garden's not worth that much attention.'

'I was just wondering what Gabrielle was looking at.'

'Well, I'm looking at you. Now turn this way and do some wondering about me.'

'She looks like a stone sentinel standing there.'

'I don't know why she worries you so much. It's as though you two share some dreadful secret.'

Weatherby tried not to show his dismay at that accurate observation, and hugged Penny to him without replying.

Suddenly an abrasive voice rang out from the adjoining orchard gate.

'I warned you, didn't I, Pen?' barked a thin-featured man in a faded brown suit which matched the colour of his insane motionless eyes.

'Frank!' screamed Penny and pulled herself in front of Weatherby.

Weatherby had completely forgotten the warnings her first husband had been regularly delivering, and it was not until he saw the revolver in his hand that he quickly changed positions with Penny. Apparently that was just what Frank wanted. Without a word of explanation he aimed the weapon at the splendid target of Weatherby's waistcoat. With cool, cruel premeditation he squeezed the trigger twice and the reports echoed about the hotel grounds. Penny was too stunned to

scream, but clung on to Weatherby as though he would be all right if he were not allowed to collapse to the ground. She was still holding on to him when every police colleague of his at the reception dinner leapt on Frank as though he were dessert. He was pinned to the ground before he could run many yards and the revolver was taken from him.

'Weatherby, Weatherby!' Penny called over his shoulder. 'Are you all right?' she asked, not daring to turn him round and look at his chest.

Weatherby leaned his head back to look at her, and replied in amazement, 'Yes Penny . . . they must have been blanks. Nothing hit me. I didn't feel a thing.'

'He must have missed you,' said Jack, running up to them, his face glowing with relief and champagne.

'Bullets could have gone anywhere.'

'But he fired at point-blank range,' Penny insisted. 'He couldn't have missed.'

'If he were sane, perhaps,' Jack reminded her. 'But I don't reckon he ever was.'

'I don't know how,' Penny gulped, 'but you're still alive.'

'Perhaps heaven wasn't ready for me,' Weatherby smiled to hide his own amazement. 'You ever heard of a black angel?'

'Fool . . .' Penny replied, recovering her composure. 'I can see I'll have to knit you a bullet proof vest.'

'I thought that waistcoat might have been bullet proof myself,' grinned Jack. 'I can't see any other explanation for it.'

'I have taste,' Weatherby told his brother-in-law. 'It may be odd taste, but Penny likes it.'

'Come back into the reception and leave those two alone, Jack,' said Connie, coming across the lawn to collect him. 'We might as well keep the party going. There are enough police here to handle Frank. He would have liked nothing more than to know he spoiled the wedding.'

'And the bridegroom,' Weatherby whispered to Penny. Over her shoulder Weatherby could see Gabrielle still

standing like a stone sentinel. She seemed to have been totally unmoved by the incident and a possible explanation for his deliverance came to him he froze.

Later Penny was obliged to spend an hour with her friends in the office at the town hall to honour a promise she had made months before. Even Weatherby was excluded, but he knew just the way he wanted to spend that hour.

The guests dispersed, and as Paula, Jack and Connie walked back to the bungalow Weatherby followed the enigmatic Gabrielle to the pebbled shore where she sat on a breakwater, waiting for him. Weatherby stayed a short distance from her as he asked, 'What happened?'

'I can't shout from here without telling the whole village. Come closer,' Gabrielle said.

Carefully he obeyed and leaned against the breakwater she was sitting on.

'You'll get your suit dirty leaning against that,' she warned him.

'I'd get even dirtier if I were to sit on there with you.'

'Well, I don't have to stay immaculate. I'm not about to have a honeymoon.' Gabrielle read the apprehension in his face. 'You aren't going to have any problems are you?'

'Goodness no. Everything functions reasonably well considering what happened to it.'

'Good. I'd hate to see Penny disappointed.'

'Aren't you going to let me have my wedding present now?' he asked.

'Oh? What did I promise you apart from the medical dictionary then?'

'You promised to explain just how you managed to save me from the ultimate operation two months ago, before some Watcher catches up with us.' When Gabrielle did not reply, he went on, 'I know you stopped those bullets as well.'

'You know about the Watchers?'

'Yes, of course. They are the ultimate Law enforcers. You'll soon be finding out about them for yourself anyway.'

'Still,' Gabrielle encouraged him, 'Go on.'

'They enforce Laws by using symbols which can be

recognised by all sophisticated life forms. If the Law isn't obeyed after one of these is issued . . .' he shrugged. 'They have more power than all the civilisations in the galaxy. They don't use it much because no one makes a habit of crossing them.' He looked at her intently as an idea struck him. 'You mean you managed to contact a Watcher?'

'Not exactly.'

'But how did you know anything about them?'

'Poor Toby might have developed the knowledge, but would have been too easily frightened to use it,' Gabrielle explained. She paused. 'Mortal or immortal life is relative to its environment, space time, or element. Spirits as humans know them are acquired by many means, the most usual being natural growth. You were an exception though. The first android to acquire a spirit.'

'But how? I don't remember it suddenly arriving.'

'It is being investigated. You were not spared because you developed a human biology, but because you somehow acquired a spirit along the way. No one knows where it came from, or if it will happen again.'

'How do you know all this, Gabrielle?' Weatherby asked.

Gabrielle casually reached out to rumple his hair, and replied, 'Because, my dear stowaway, I am a Watcher.'

JOANNA RUSS
EXTRA (ORDINARY) PEOPLE

A brand-new collection of fiction and fantasy from one of the most significant writers ever to emerge from the field of science fiction.

The heroic resistance of a mediaeval abbess who resolves to defend her community when a Viking invasion sails up the river ... the adventures of two mysterious passengers aboard a nineteenth century clipper ship bound for America ... a time-travelling heroine disguised as a male God on an errand of mercy in a barbaric past ... a Gothic tale of intrigue and romance between two women.

Joanna Russ once more draws on her talent for vivid characterisation to involve us in worlds not our own, exploring power relationships in past and future to illuminate our own time.

'Souls', the first narrative in *Extra (Ordinary) People*, won a Hugo Award in 1983, *The Science Fiction Chronicle*'s award for the best novella of 1983, and the *Locus* readers' poll for best novella of 1983.

First British publication

sf

0 7043 3940 1
£1.95

SALLY MILLER GEARHART
THE WANDERGROUND

'Machines outside the city, continued Evona, were working no better than usual. Breakdowns were still consistent — planes faltered after less than an hour's flight, trains and autos ground to a stop after short bursts of speed, sails and oars were still the only means of progress over water ... communication with any other surviving city was limited to runners.'

Picture a world where the Earth itself has rebelled against the domination of men — they survive within the cities, but outside them technology, from tractors to guns, fails to operate. But many women have escaped, and within their own communities in the hill country of the Wanderground have developed astonishing physical and mental powers — telepathy, telekinesis, even the power of flight. Now rumours abound that changes within the city may soon affect the lives of the hill women.

The Wanderground provides a Utopian vision of the future that will entertain and exhilarate.

'Sally Gearhart is an original and so is her book. Buy it. Read it. Give it to a friend.' Rita Mae Brown.

First British publication

sf

0 7043 3947 1
£1.95

JANE PALMER
THE PLANET DWELLER

The Mott were the most greedy and power-mad species in the universe. With the help of the brilliant engineer Kulp and the space distort net he had invented, they planned to drive the planet creatures from their homes in their search for new worlds to possess. Fortunately an escape route was at hand for the Planet Dweller – an escape route which threatened the future of the Earth. It is left to Diana, a middle-aged mother who hears voices, Yuri, the eccentric and drunken scientist, and several large furry animals with luminous pink eyes, to outwit the Mott and save the Earth, though they may have to travel half-way across the universe to do it . . .

The Planet Dweller is a witty and fast-moving fantasy which combines all the best elements of science fiction with Jane Palmer's unique gift for characterisation and strong sense of the absurd. Hers is a truly fresh voice in the science fiction field.

First publication

sf

0 7043 3948 X
£1.95

JOANNA RUSS
THE FEMALE MAN

'A visionary novel about a society where women can do all we now fantasize in closets and kitchens and beds ... intricate, witty, furious, savage'   Marge Piercy

'A sophisticated work' *Sunday Times*

'A book women can read with glee' *City Limits*

The Female Man extends the boundaries of science fiction. It explores language and sexuality, customs and conventions, dreams and nightmares. It provides a witty and subversive analysis of the power men hold over women in our society.

sf

0 7043 3949 8
£1.95

THE ADVENTURES OF ALYX

Alyx – assassin, thief, hired bodyguard
Alyx – courageous, cunning and loyal to her own interests
Alyx – professional picklock, dragonslayer and wit
Alyx – 'among the wisest of a sex that is surpassingly wise'

The Adventures of Alyx are witty, serious, entertaining and profound. Alyx is a heroine beyond our wildest dreams.

sf

0 7043 3972 2
£1.95

JEN GREEN & SARAH LEFANU,
Editors
DESPATCHES FROM THE FRONTIERS
OF THE FEMALE MIND
An Anthology of Original Stories

A collection of startling new science fiction stories from
well-known authors, including Zoë Fairbairns, Mary Gentle,
Gwyneth Jones, Tanith Lee, Naomi Mitchison, Joanna Russ,
Josephine Saxton, Alice Sheldon, Lisa Tuttle, Pamela Zoline;
and introducing new writers Lannah Battley, Penny Casdagli,
Margaret Elphinstone, Frances Gapper, Beverley Ireland,
Pearlie McNeill, Sue Thomason.

This collection comes from the frontiers and offers a glimpse
of what lies beyond.

sf

0 7043 3973 0
£2.50

JODY SCOTT
PASSING FOR HUMAN

Introducing Benaroya, a well meaning hedonist from Inter-
stellar Station B, who visits Earth in a number of guises
including Emma Peel, Virginia Woolf, and Brenda Starr. Her
mission: to sow wild oats, save Earth from alien invasion,
sort out the human race and generally have a good time.

With an all-star cast, including Abraham Lincoln, Einstein,
Heidi's Grandfather, General George S. Patton, The Prince
of Darkness, The Royal Canadian Mounted Police, Ancient
Egypt, and several hundred Richard Nixons . . .

'What Paganini did to four strings and three-and-a-half
octaves, Jody Scott does for our dear, undead genre'
Barry N Malzberg

sf

0 7043 3990 0
£2.50

JOSEPHINE SAXTON
QUEEN OF THE STATES

'If you would like to dance hand in hand with a delightfully sympathetic, mad – or perhaps totally not mad – companion, this is your book. Highly recommended, especially to gourmets' Naomi Mitchison

Magdalen is on her own planet and out to lunch, weaving through the fantasies of those around her. She moves through time and space, from a private mental hospital to an alien spaceship where she is interrogated about the function of human sexual behaviour.

Is Magdalen mad, or have the aliens really landed? A brilliant original novel from this well known and loved British science fiction writer, author of *The Power of Time* (short stories, 1985) and four previous SF novels including *The Travails of Jane Saint and Other Stories* (The Women's Press, 1986).

0 7043 3992 7
£1.95